Children of the Waters

Modern Middle East
Literatures in Translation Series

Children of the Waters

Ibtihal Salem

Translated from the Arabic
by
Marilyn Booth

The Center for Middle Eastern Studies
The University of Texas at Austin

Library of Congress Catalogue Card Number: 2002111854
ISBN: 0-292-77773-6

Printed in the United States of America

Cover painting by Gazbia Sirry, Cairo, Egypt.

Cover design: Diane Watts

Series editor: Annes McCann-Baker

Acknowledgements

I am grateful to Sahar Tawfiq, Sharif Elmusa, and Annes McCann-Baker for their encouragement, their careful readings, and their fine suggestions. I thank Ibtihal Salem for her patience and her readiness to laugh. And I recall with fond delight the many hours of conversation about writing and life, and the many pots of tea and plates of *ful* that I've shared with her over the past fifteen years.

Marilyn Booth
Urbana, Illinois, U.S.A.
November 2001

Contents

Children of the Waters

Introduction

Ibtihal Salem's writing offers an anchorage—to borrow one of her own motifs—from which to regard Egyptian writing today. Over nearly thirty years of her writing life, she has moved toward what the eminent novelist, poet, and critic Idwar al-Kharrat has called "writing across genres." Her meteoric stories hover somewhere between the narrative demands of story-telling, the immediacy and visuality of vignettes or film takes, and the compressed depths of prose poetry. Salem's writings are difficult to classify. She is not alone in this experimentation, of course; prose poetry, for example, is a popular form of writing among Egypt's literary avant-garde now. Salem's writings evoke a literary ferment in Egypt today that is producing an outpouring of intriguing cross-genre writing. Balancing social messages and textual experimentation in varying ways, the thirty-five texts in this collection span Salem's career to date, from the early 1970s to the close of the 1990s.

Ibtihal Salem's writing reminds us of how visible women are on the Arabic literary scene, and this volume joins a growing body of writing by Arab women available in English translation. In Salem's writing "generation"—those who began to write and publish in the 1970s—as well as in the two-and-a-half literary "generations" of Arab creative writers that have followed, women are prominent voices, as novelists, short story writers, poets, playwrights, and critics. Salem's stories bespeak the centrality of gender in the cultural construction of Egyptian identities and experience(s) today. Most of her stories link the pressures of poverty to experiences of gender marginality—as Vivian Gornick, in another context, has put it with an edgy lucidity, "the damnable injustice of being born inside a body categorically destined for exclusion from the world enterprise."[1] Yet, the women of Salem's stories—who range in age from early adolescence to the end of a long life—celebrate the heritages that have shaped their identities as much as they resist aspects of them.

Salem accomplishes this critical celebration by rewriting the Egyptian folk tale, and the long history of women's storytelling, in "Songs from the Tree's Core," "Passages," "Palm Trees and the Sea," and other stories. She is not alone, for interest in the *turath*, "the heritage," whether of popular and folk cultures or of the high literary and religious tradition, underlies the literary strategies of many writers in Egypt today, women and men, new writers and seasoned ones. Recently, Salem has pursued this interest in a different vein by writing stories for children, creating new "folk tales" for a new generation.

Concerned with communicating across generations, in her writings Salem also explores generational difference as a thematic and structural foundation for narrative. A young protagonist—an adolescent or a young married woman—will try to resist the social burdens that older women have chosen to take on and negotiate. Yet in Salem's stories, the younger woman's "negotiation" encompasses the gap between a resistant internal monologue and an outward silence. She resists, but her muteness reminds us of the strong pull of social compliance. The young girl in "February" cannot speak to her mother openly of her desires. Her resistance is physical, but it is also silent. The young mother in "Behind Closed Doors" knows the pressures of an extended family of in-laws; and it is she, rather than her wayward, husband who must bear family "honor" on her shoulders and preserve social pretense. Or, Salem's protagonists may be slightly older mothers, observing painfully the consequences of poverty on children without choices. Distance and silence may characterize the relationship, but—as in "Work Gang"—there is also unspoken connection, support and sympathy from those around, and a quiet, agonized love tested but not broken in hardship.

Indeed, for Salem writing is affirmation as much as it is critique. Both qualities mark the writing act as essential to her selfhood. She has said that—

> writing creates a kind of psychological balance in the face of the many social, political, and economic transformations [that we are encountering in Egypt now].... For me, writing has long represented an exquisite sense of existence, beauty and self-realization. When I distance myself from writing for any length of time, I become frustrated and mentally confused. When I return to it I

4

feel as if I've been born anew. Sometimes when I finish writing a story I take a long breath, comb my hair, and put on my nicest clothes, as if it is a holiday. These are simple moments of joy that make me feel as if I deserve to live.[2]

But her stories do not romanticize the world that they affirm. Salem is particularly skilled at interweaving the perspectives of young and old, of listening to the world through children's ears and then bringing the adult world to bear upon that sensitivity. Her stories thus open questions that Egyptians today cannot ignore. What happens to moral frameworks when there is no money for food? How do material pressures shape, and stifle, creativity? What is the future for a demoralized middle class? Why does "woman" become the symbolic receptacle of social order and honor? And— a vital thread winding through modern Arabic literature—how does the continuing failure to satisfy Palestinian national aspirations permeate the everyday lives of millions of not only Palestinians but also Arabs through-out the region? Attending to contemporary global politics in a few stories, Salem suggests how the ongoing fallout from the Gulf War can become an agonizing and humiliating detail of mundane existence. In "My Friend Patriot" and "Fire," the hovering presence of Katyushas and Patriots be-comes one dimension in a character's struggle to define self and future. In today's world, the ways that global politics contour personal selfhood and collective identities, which we ignore at our peril, must enter the domain of the short story.

Born in 1949 in Egypt's capital city, Ibtihal Salem is a child of Cairo. But at the heart of her identity as an Egyptian lie the waters of sea and river: the Nile—Egypt's lifegiver as Herodotus declared so long ago—the Mediterranean, the Suez Canal, the Red Sea. After graduating from Ain Shams University in Cairo with a B.A. in psychology, Salem went to live in Port Saïd, native city of the husband she had met at the university and the setting of many of her short stories. Sitting astride the Canal and the Mediterranean Sea, Port Saïd has been a busy entrepot since the mid-nine-teenth century when the Suez Canal was constructed. Geographical and historical continuity surface in the city's late twentieth-century manifesta-tion, for it is Egypt's first duty-free zone. A story that appears elsewhere in translation, "City of Cardboard," summons Port Saïd's blend of free-port capitalism, sailors' haven, and lower-middle-class Egyptian daily life to portray the currents of Egypt's national economy in the mid-1980s. Booming for some with its new emphasis on imports of luxury goods, that economy was leaving many others behind. It is a prescient story, given the further developments of the last century's final decade as so glitteringly visible in Cairo's well-lit facades now.[3]

Salem lives part of the time in October City, one of the "new towns" ringing Cairo through which the Egyptian government has tried to practice an urban version of desert reclamation, and part of the time in Giza, still home to the Pyramids but also a densely-occupied Cairo suburb. Yet, she continues to travel to Port Saïd and to other coastal towns, whence she has drawn much of her literary energy. Port Saïd, though, is also the hub of a difficult past: a war front, a family split by war injuries and underground political work, a child born in conditions of internal exile, and a constant reminder of both the colonialism and the cosmopolitan merchant activity that have marked Egypt's near past. Salem's novel *Blue Windows* (*Nawafidh zarqa'*, Cairo, 2000) takes up this history. This novel, her first, won third place in the 1998 "Literature of the October War" Egypt-wide competition. In *Blue Windows,* the forces that have shaped Port Saïd—and Egypt—sculpt the extraordinary outlook of a young female protagonist who thinks of herself as a male, and refers to herself as "him." For the socially prescribed attributes of femininity cannot represent her story of political activism, personal separation and loss, hunger and desire, and connection. In the company of other writers of her generation who have moved from the short story to the novel in recent years—Siham Bayyumi, Sahar Tawfiq, Radwa Ashur, Selwa Bakr—Salem's novel relates a memoir of social memory rooted in the recent history of Egypt.

Ibtihal Salem's short stories emerge from that sense of social memory and collective responsibility, too. Like those other writers, Salem is not afraid to explore the dangers of identity-based political agendas in a society where economic hardship fuels mutual antagonisms as well as mutual support. Boldly, she alludes to the power wielded by various kinds of authority, especially in her stories about school-age girls. This is the stuff of controversy. Was it coincidental that a sentence mentioning the presence of a priest handing out treats to children was omitted from "Bags of Candy" when it appeared in Arabic? For the little Muslim girl thinks she must borrow a name that is identifiably Christian if she is to get her bag of candy from the priest.

Sectarian identities of any sort are a sensitive topic, even as most Muslims and Copts in Egypt live amicably together. Salem points out the disciplinary force of ideologies *whatever* their content in other stories. In "Rage," a walled private school run by priests and nuns has its own set of hierarchies into which the pupil is trained. Many Egyptians of Salem's age and class, Muslim and Christian, have attended these private religious schools, receiving their early education in French more than in Arabic. Where lies the source of a returning schoolgirl's alienation? In religious difference? Or in a history of colonization? Or elsewhere? And how do gender hierarchies fuel "Rage"? In "Bags of Candy," too, the authority of the school to define and divide people receives support from the patriarchal hierarchy of the family. "Pangs" alludes quietly to the divisions and communities wrought by politics and sacrifice, evoking a history of political activism that Salem's generation, as university students, experienced. Whether in Port Saïd at the tip of the Suez Canal, Cairo on the Nile, Alexandria on the Mediterranean, or elsewhere, Egyptians have fought on many fronts for internal justice and sovereignty over a land that so many outsiders have sought to control.

Waters mark the very different socioeconomic communities that Egypt holds, too: Nile fishermen and peasants, seafarers and the urban civil servants who make their insufficient livings in the mass of wealth and poverty that shapes the Cairene Nile skyline today, the Mediterranean from across which come many of the patterns of consumption reflected in Cairo's neon. Salem's narratives range across these Egyptian lives: moments, individuals, the dying elderly and the starving but playing child, the teenaged girl and the single mother, the bedroom, the garden, the street, the Catholic missionary girls' school, the printing house. The moments she crafts are anything but isolated from the society-wide political and economic shifts that have left many in Egypt desperate, unable to imagine a future or hold onto a decent present:

> Writing is also intense pain. For instance, I'm from the generation [that grew up with] Nasser: I opened my eyes upon joyful dreams and fantastic ambitions. I continued to dream; to read, to imagine a better and more welcoming world through the stages of childhood and adolescence—until I was slapped by the Catastrophe of 1967. It shook me like an earthquake, yanked me apart

from the tree [of my identity]. I saw with my own eyes the destruction of my early dreams and the hurt was born inside of
me.... writing was the best, maybe the only, support as I tried to
stand up again. I learned how art that is beautiful can also emerge
from great pain.[4]

If today's young writers are known for an extreme social alienation
expressed in fiercely internalized writing where the outside world drops
away completely, writers of "the 70s generation" like Salem continue to
confront directly through their writing the social forces that most of their
countrywomen and countrymen cannot avoid. Often poetic in its compressed language, Salem's writing is rooted in and expressive of the politics
of life in Egypt.

Born into a middle-class urban professional family, Ibtihal Salem re-
tains the far-flung ties that still bind many Egyptian urbanites to the fields
of the Delta and Upper Egypt. Her mother, a villager, raised her to value
village practices and to be comfortable with the colloquial Arabic of a world
far removed from the urban university where Salem's father taught. Her
language juxtaposes the sayings of peasant women newly uprooted from
the village with the punning possibilities of a language known for laughter;
and this language poses the in-your-face tones of Egypt's fast-growing, young
nouveaux riche class against the echoes of Arabic artistic traditions, from
storytelling to the highly formal poetry that shaped an early Arab literary
identity. In "February" the image of the small, round, firm, and yellow
lupine bean, *tirmis*, a popular street snack in Egypt, is a down-to-earth
aunt's metaphor for her little niece's budding breasts. But it yields in the
aunt's colorful language to the more "adult" pomegranate, that might bring
to mind both the metaphoric fecundity and sensuality of the Arabic ode,
and also contemporary Arabic pop culture that bears some echoes of folk
expression. If *tirmis* beans are so familiar as to breed contempt, pomegranates are the sensual future! Yellow to red, hard to soft, mild to tart, plain to
sophisticated: color, taste, texture, and symbolic weight communicate a
girl's growing up as they evoke shared cultural symbols. In "Passage" and
in "Songs from the Tree's Core" Salem draws on the storytelling traditions
that have given the world the richness of the *Thousand and One Nights*,
and on the lyrics of childhood songs, to speak about both the shaping and
the liberating potential of a storytelling imaginary that draws on a rich

cultural past. With these cultural valences and linguistic compressions, Salem is not always easy to read, nor do her stories provide quick closure. Indeed, as noted novelist and critic Edwar al-Kharrat said in a study written for Salem's first published collection, most of her stories have "endings open to the horizons, to the unknown, to the value of withdrawal, freedom, new embarkations...."[5] The same adventurous openness is true of her latest work, a novel in progress that traces the difficult exiles and transnational odysseys of two hopeful young people, trying to maintain the positive identity of Arab in a world that obstructs multiple possibilities.

After a decade in Port Saïd, Ibtihal Salem returned to Cairo. Since then she has worked as a translator (French to Arabic) for the state's radio and television agencies and as an assistant director in one of Cairo's public-sector theaters. Widely published in Egyptian and other Arabic-language periodicals, she has brought out three short story collections: *al-Nawras* (The Gull, 1989), *Dunya saghira* (Small World, 1992), and *Nakhb iktimal al-qamar* (A Toast to the Full Moon, 1997), from which most of the stories translated here are selected.

In the present political climate, writers in Egypt—particularly women—may face censure or censorship for openly expressing critical attitudes about the interrelations of everyday life, national policies, and constraints imposed as well as possibilities opened by Egypt's implication in the global processes of twentieth-century existence. Poverty, unemployment, and curbs on labor organization; restraints on free expression and public behavior imposed in the name of religious community; taboos around sexuality and sexual freedom—all are realities of everyday life that today's writers address. Like some others, Ibtihal says she cannot publish all of her stories. Like many other women writing in the Arab world now, she believes it essential to write female sexuality into the equations of fulfillment and frustration that mark daily life on every level. Yet, as pen-wielding women across time and cultures have repeatedly discovered, they are attacked and denigrated for writing sexuality, especially through the all-too-familiar (and not culture specific!) tactic of branding women's writings as necessarily, transparently, and damningly "autobiographical."

Ibtihal Salem's stories are not easy to read, or to translate. Their sharp juxtapositions, kaleidoscopic colloquial language, compressed descriptions, and open endings may not appeal to those who seek "sociological" satisfaction in writings translated from the Arab world. Her vignettes capture moments and situations with a suddenness that may be puzzling to readers from outside the society. Because of that, and with Ibtihal's approval and help, I provide brief introductory observations for each story, often drawn from conversations with Ibtihal. These are new; they were not part of the stories' original Arabic contexts. I also incorporate explanations of terms and usages unfamiliar to speakers of English. Through this intervention, I try to set the scene for the reader and at the same time bring reader and writer closer together, while hoping that these fleeting prefaces can fire rather than stifle imaginative readings. It is not easy to enter another world. But I hope and believe this journey to be worthwhile. In the company of generations of writers in Egypt, Ibtihal Salem gives life to the lives bounded by Egypt's waters.

NOTES

¹Vivian Gornick, "Wildman" (review of J. Raskin, *For the Hell of It: The Life and Times of Abbie Hoffman*), *The Nation*, January 6, 1997, p. 27.

²Ibtihal Salem, "Lahzat farah," *Majallat al-Hadath* (Kuwait) 20 (March 1998), p. 14.

³Ibtihal Salem, "City of Cardboard," in Marilyn Booth, ed. and trans., *My Grandmother's Cactus: Stories by Egyptian Women* (London: Quartet, 1991), pp. 98-104.

⁴Ibtihal Salem, "Lahzat farah," p. 14.

⁵Edwar al-Kharrat, "Dirasa: Hadhihi al-majmu`a wa-ta'ir al-shi`r al-`anid," pp. 113-138 in Ibtihal Salem, *Al-Nawras* (Cairo: al-Hay'a al-misriyya al-`amma lil-kitab, Ser. Ishraqat adabiyya 39, 1989), quote, p. 136.

Arabi

"*Port Saïd was a city divided in two. There was the* Hayy al-ifranj *(foreigners' quarter) and the* Hayy al-'arab *(Arabs' quarter). Among the foreigners lived wealthy Egyptians, too. The poor were not allowed into the foreigners' quarter, and, when children tried to steal into the* Hayy al-ifranj, *the police would have to return them. Feelings of resentment grew especially after the 1956 Tripartite Aggression against Egypt, and they were expressed in nationalist slogans. "Al-Arabi" (the Arab) thus meant "someone belonging to us, someone from our quarter." The man's name could be anything—often it was Sayyid—but this would become a sort of added nickname: 'Sayyid ya Arabi!' But then with* infitah *(see preface to "Making Bets"), the age of consumption and smuggling came to Port Saïd, and with it a spirit of opportunism that replaced that sense of collective belonging. I've lived these transformations, I have seen them all in Port Saïd.*" (Ibtihal Salem)

Like many of Ibtihal Salem's stories, the following one relies on colloquial expressions, usages, and proverbs. That Umm Rida (mother of Rida) wears shibshib Zannuba *(Zaynab sandals or flipflops) as opposed to* shibshib Khadiga *(Khadiga sandals or ones with a solid band over the front of the foot) and that this very colloquial term characterizes her, sets her immediately into a specific (low) socioeconomic slot for Egyptian readers. Egyptian Arabic conveys morning greetings with beautiful, lush metaphoric phrases: "morning of sweet cream," "morning of light," and the like. That Arabi greets the mayor with a sardonic* sabahayn wa-sardina *(two good mornings and a sardine) reminds us that historically the economic roots of this community were in fishing, but juxtaposed with Arabi's desperation, the phrase also re-*

minds us that times have changed, and the fishing community's for-
tunes have turned. Social hierarchies remain strong echoes through the
use of a pre-1952 (pre-revolution) title, bey, traditionally a wealthy,
well-connected pillar of the establishment. The mayor's use of the title
sitt (lady) a respectable mode of address to a matron, seems ironic in
the circumstances. *

---

* The translator's prefaces to the stories will combine quotes from the author, drawn from the author's conversations with the translator, and contextual observations.

H e hurled his shirt into the open air at the very moment the ferry bumped the dock.

All eyes shifted between sky and earth, gazes measuring the distance between the circle of people below and the head turned downward from atop a tall expanse of steel.

The ambulance siren fused with the blast of the ferry as policemen converged on the lighthouse tower. The circle widened with an advancing army of onlookers. The stars on the shoulders of the harbor district chief sparkled as he put a microphone to his mouth.

"Come on down, Arabi. We'll talk about it down here."

The faraway voice came like a thin whistle.

"My blessings come from the bounty of God. I'm not budging. If there's a tough guy among you, let him come up here. I'm rooted here 'til we see the end of it."

Policemen were spreading across the harbor pavement. Gestures of helplessness filled the air, as people struck their palms together dubiously. But when the trousers came flying—a huge, black, flapping crow among seagulls—groans mounted from the crowd.

"For the last time I'm warning you, Arabi. Come down, or else…"

Arabi's response was to lean his body over the metal wall at the very top of the lighthouse column and scream.

"You, world out there, you people you, ten years it's been, rats in our bedrooms, garbage for neighbors, and all the flies, in a nest made of tin. Yes, ten years drinking nothing but gall."

Growls and mutters replaced the quiet breathing below, and the jostling clamor grew just below the tower. Here and there a shout managed to slip out, freeing itself into the air.

"World of sinners, unbelievers. They stay on the backs of the poor until they break them."

"The fellow is having his say. It's true, the world doesn't care."

"To God alone is all power and might! The guy's off his head, he's gone, and all we can do is stand here and watch."

Police swarmed everywhere now, just like the ubiquitous flies, blocking the passage of bicycles and cars toward the ferry. The crowd was massing, and all eyes were fixed upward.

He stripped off the yellowing undershirt and tossed it from the top of the lighthouse. It fell onto the upturned face of one of the policemen ranged along the harbor wall.

"Come on, over here, in front of me, at the tower." One of the policemen was shouting as he shoved at the back of a woman who was already approaching the place at a gallop. Her hair hung loose over her full body, and she could not quite keep her balance, stumbling on the worn out *zannuba* flipflops she wore. The police chief stalked over to her.

"D'you know exactly what you're going to do?"

"Yes, yes, sure, *bey*."

She took the microphone cautiously from his hand. She raised her head, blinked, and lowered it quickly.

"What is it? What now?"

"The sun's blistering, *bey*."

A nearby detective clapped her shoulder roughly as he shouted. "Hurry up, let's get this over with, the *bey* doesn't have all day."

She raised her head, eyes half-closed, and put the microphone right on her mouth. Her voice trembled.

15

"Arabi, now come on down, God help you." The voice seemed to fragment in the air and no answer came.

"Go on. Say everything you were going to say, *Sitt* Umm ..."

"Umm Rida, *bey*."

"Go on, then, Umm Rida." There was no patience left in the police chief's voice.

"He's not answering, *bey*."

The detective shoved her hard in the back as he shouted. "Listen to what the *bey* says, go on."

She threw the microphone from her hand and clutched at one of the slender tower's smooth steel columns, trying helplessly to give it a shake as she gazed upward.

"Come on, man, use your brain, come down now, you've left me all on my own."

The crowd was still and silent, waiting for an answer from Arabi. But none came. Umm Rida turned and pushed the detective away from her body with both hands.

"Get out of my way, you. He comes down, he doesn't. I don't care! He can throw his old self right into hell! I've left the children all alone without any food, and by now the little fellow'll be crying so hard, my little darling, he'll taste nothing but the bitterness."

As she hurried off toward the ferry, the police chief hurried after her.

"And Arabi?..."

"*In sha' Allah,* God willing, he'll break his neck, aren't we poor enough as it is? I mean, bless his wicked little heart, what help was he anyway?"

The police chief stood still. He ordered his men to leave Arabi's wife alone to go on her way. The crowd looked on warily as whistles sounded, like sparks of fire catching in the depths of the sweaty tumult. The wind pitched the last cry of a sacrificial lamb over the scene, after Umm Rida had gone.

"How many times I've tried with that lad Amin, son of the barber at the end of the street! I can't take it any more. He'd write a complaint for me, trying to get us a place to live, even a shack out of two-by-fours on a heap of ruins. And the one who says 'tomorrow' and the one who says 'the day after,' and the one who says God knows what.... One year drags in the next, and like the proverb says, 'Even the guy who makes noise won't survive.'"

The senior officer signaled to his troops to go in. Batons swinging, they moved yelling into the crowd. "Make room, buddy, c'mon, you there, and you! Everyone to your own business, now, his honor the chief is speaking to him, he'll convince the guy."

"Convince who, old fellow! You guys just want to get us, you think anything you say can fool us." A policeman wheeled on the speaker, swinging his stick. Policemen, people, everyone fighting, hands, sticks, stones, until their chief shot his gun into the air and, frightened, folks scattered every which way. The murmuring lessened as some folks moved back, seeing the police lining up with weapons brandished high.

The sound of the ferry motor approached, and a black vehicle rolled onto the asphalt, a small flag flapping on its front. Whispers were flying back and forth.

The mayor, himself. He's here. In person.

"Not only that, the security chief is with him."

"That's the way they are. They don't show up except to show us the red eye, they just want to scare us with their bluster. Poor guy, *yaa wildaah*, the chap's brain has gone clear out of his head."

The policemen shuffled into position to salute. The police chief brought the microphone to his lips.

"Listen to what I have to say, Arabi. The mayor is here, himself, and he promises he'll take care of your problem if you come down."

Arabi peered out from the top, to see for himself that the mayor was indeed there. When he spoke his voice was hoarse.

"*Sabaahayn wa-sardina*, sir! I've been trying for years to crawl into your shadow, mister. I'm a dead man today if I don't get a key to an apartment like other folks have."

He ripped off his baggy cotton undergarment and there he was, naked as the day his mother brought him into the world. Just as skinny, just as weak as that long-ago newborn, no more solid than a thin black thread separating earth and sky. He opened his legs and the pee ran down the burning metal, to blend with its rusty surface. The police chief wiped his forehead with the back of his hand, muttering an inaudible curse. The mayor, stiff in his dark suit, his shoes gleaming, took the microphone from the police chief's hand. People seemed to stop breathing, so still it was, and the challenge mirrored in their eyes grew darker.

"Arabi, son, listen to me, hear me out. I give you my vow that I'll give you the key as soon as you come down."

Arabi was spinning, spinning naked in the tiny space at the tower's top. The mayor took a silver key out of his pocket and raised it high, turning it this way and that to catch the sun's rays. The flashes courted Arabi's gaze, wooing him, enticing him. He put out his foot to climb down, but just as quickly he drew it back.

"Swear in front of everyone," he shouted hoarsely. The mayor gave a sharp nod. "I swear." The security chief at his side saw his chance and grabbed the microphone from him.

"Believe us, Arabi, come on, show some manners! Don't destroy everything; you've got a whole heap of flesh at home to take care of. Come on down and we'll work this out together."

Arabi put his foot on the top step of the spiral staircase inside the open tower crowned by huge searchlights. His emaciated body seemed to grow longer and longer the further down he came, and his bones jutted out ever more sharply. When he was almost down to the wide base of the tower, the order went out to two of the policemen to go and meet him. One of them mounted the two steps that joined the base to the spiral staircase, while the other waited below. The first one grabbed Arabi around the middle with one hand and encircled his torso with the other. "You gave us a real run-around, son of a bitch," the policeman snapped at him, pushing him roughly toward his mate, who welcomed him with slaps to his face and chest. The policeman's two thick hands grabbed and squeezed Arabi's thin arms, dragging him along the ground toward the captain. He threw Arabi under the feet of the police chief, ignoring his screams completely. The chief fired a few shots in the air to scatter the people who had begun to close in around them, but some of them grabbed at the policemen while others slung rocks from a distance. The police chief began kicking Arabi in the face and chest, until bruises swelled up across his body and blood ran from his mouth. The mayor bustled over to his black *khanzira*—the huge Mercedes the townsfolk called derisively "the hog"— and busied himself getting in. He turned back and shouted in the direction of the chief.

"Take that dog away and teach him a good, long lesson." People started to run after the car, cursing. The police worked to hold them back, and the stones flew from hands raised high. An old man tried to squeeze himself into the circle of besiegers who had tightened around Arabi. He yanked off his threadbare vest and threw it over the bruised and naked body, spitting out oaths all the while.

"Dirty sons of bitches. If they swore on water in the desert, it would turn to ice."

"Arabi"
Port Saïd, 1984
Al-Nawras, pp. 75-85

Anticipation

"I detest the state of waiting. Time, passing, intensifies one's emotions, both joy and bitterness; and when waiting grows longer, anticipation yields doubt and unease. In a port city, any port city, you will find women waiting. In a harbor, any harbor, they wait: for ferries, boats, ships, sailors. They say goodbye not knowing when their men will return. This is the existence of the Mediterranean, all the way around. Women, waiting. "

She opened the window partway. The glass-fronted houses rebuffed her as the suffocating night drove her back. Drops of salt wet her lips and dove straight to a heart made heavy by the cold and the waiting.

The rays of the lighthouse flash past like lightning. The dogs' barking cleaves the street's blackness, and her eyes, hiding behind the window panel, lie in wait for the screech of a bicycle that only she recognizes, when it arrives with the very last ferry.

The lone kiosk on the corner has its shutters down and locked. A gust of wind spins the empty cans, and cats play in the garbage of the street. The women clinging to the rusty light-posts scatter. A security patrol storms the silence, and a conscript calls out. "Who's there?"

There's no one there but me, she sighed. Me, nighttime, and the silence. The ships' horns are taking their leave, bound for foreign places. The ferry's beam breaks through the heart of the dew as the screech of the bicycle that no one else knows sounds from far away, grinding the loose stones on the asphalt. That shrill voice comes nearer, and then nearer, to trample on the face whose glimmer flickers out with the first rap on the door.

"Taraqqub"
Cairo, 1994
Majallat al-Katiba no. 7, June/July 1994, p. 35
Nakhb iktimal al-qamar, pp. 23-25

Behind Closed Doors

"In our society there are always closed doors. They carry many meanings, especially for women and girls. They mean concealment, emotions held inside. They signal the things that happen within any home. Men, too, hide and protect themselves behind closed doors. There is no space in which to talk about sexuality, about feelings. We must rebel against this; we must force open those closed doors."

Haagga is literally the title of a woman who has accomplished the pilgrimage to Mecca, as all able Muslims are enjoined to do sometime during their lives. The term is used colloquially as a respectful term of address to older women, as its equivalent, hagg, *refers to older men.*

Proverbs are the salt of colloquial Arabic, perhaps especially in women's speech. Many, many Arabic proverbs allude to abiding concepts of gender relations. Here, two proverbs resonate against each other and also signal generational differences in attitude. "Putting your trust in men is like putting water in a sieve." "Birds fly away but they come back to their nests." As in this story, all that needs to be said among the women is a proverb's first few words, and everyone understands. This also highlights the closeness of family—sometimes an oppressive closeness, where marriage relationships may become everyone's business.

If only the walls could talk. Her mind wandered as her eyes veered between the shut door and the wall. A relative of his brother's wife, he would tell her, had informed him that the Haagga was not very well. He would say he'd visited her, had stopped by his friend's

house afterward, and had found him in a tight spot, and then ...
and so on, and on...

Threads of steam rose from the platter of rice. Time passed
slowly, heavily: the eyes of an eagle in wait, searching.

"Come now, take some," urged the Haagga. "The food will get
cold."

She lowered her eyes. "No, I have to wait for him. Go ahead,
please. Enjoy it in good health."

His older sister smacked her lips as she tore a round of bread in
half.

"You'll find he's just off on a cloud somewhere," she remarked.
"You know what they say—'Putting your trust in men—'" The
Haagga cut her off, a frown on her face.

"Birds fly all over, but then they return to their nests."

She left with a promise to visit again soon.

She turned the key in the door. Rang the bell. Pounded on the
door.

He slid open the bolt. He was in his underwear. The sweat was
thick on his face and his eyes were unsteady.

She knew a rat when she smelled one. She headed into the
bedroom, her voice loud behind her. "Everyone was asking about
you at the Haagga's."

Her gaze lit on a pair of shoes under the bed. Dull silver, spike
heels. Her eyes traveled around the room and out to the corridor.
He followed her, making an attempt to shove one arm into a
shirtsleeve. He pressed his body against hers and laid his hand firmly
on her shoulder.

"Sh' we go out? Would you like that?"

She slipped away from him. She sensed an unfamiliar fragrance
coming from the kitchen and pushed the door open. Dusky skin,

the face of a child, bare feet. There the girl was, crouched between the door and the wall.

She rushed forward but he yanked her back. By the time she could struggle free, the concealed one had already run out of the house, shoes under her arm.

He took stock of the determination in the eyes leveled at him. "Hey, so what's the big deal? Are you doing without anything? You eat well, you have plenty of tea to drink, you get lots of sleep— so, come on, say something! Why aren't you answering?"

The earth spun, grew blurry. The strands of steam curling up from the rice platter seemed to halt, to freeze in midair. With a sigh she got to her feet. She looked into the mirror, its rim buckling with rust. She touched the white strands on either side of her face.

In the bathroom she gathered all of the laundry into a pile. Going into the kitchen, she collected plates and glasses. She scrubbed the pots and shallow metal bowls so hard that she practically wore them through, as she remembered what her mother had said.

"So is the boy his son or ours? Get him out of here—take the lad to *him*." The woman's hollering drew sparks that flew from her eyes.

"Mama, it's the dead of night. We'll sleep on it, see how things look tomorrow morning."

She could see the veins flare in her mother's clenched face.

"No 'sleeping on it,' no 'tomorrow morning.' He won't stay the night here, I said—that means he won't stay the night here."

He was perched on top of his suitcase. Leaning his little head back against the wall, he was trying hard not to close his eyes.

She pushed him, so that he would walk ahead of her. "Get up now, let's go."

The coils of steam dwindled and faded to nothing above the platter of rice.

"Nobody said she had to clear out," he yelled amidst the throng planted in the living room.

Words died in her heart.

The well-meaning folks, the Haagga, the relatives: they all stepped in. They worked to convince her and the boy to stay on with him under one roof. It was the protection of families, they said. The nighttime, they said, and what goes on behind closed doors.

She abandoned the platter of rice, a corpse on the table. She flung herself across the cold bed. She felt the light creep of his feet and then the glaring yellowness hit her eyes. The light went out in her heart.

He sat on the edge of the bed, untying his shoelaces.

"One of my brother's in-laws, he told me the Haagga was in a pretty bad way, and —"

She fled the room but his voice still came.

"I stopped by to see my buddy, found him in a tight spot—"

The turning hands of the clock surrounded her. She clamped her teeth together. Her eyes shifted between the closed door and the wall, and gazed at the time that divided the two of them, the years that sat ready to pounce.

"Khalfa al-abwab"
Cairo, 1993
Nakhb iktimal al-qamar, pp. 61-66

Making Bets

The rapid economic transitions that Egypt has seen in the last quarter century have been hard for all but a few. President Anwar Sadat's policy of Infitah, or "opening" (often called "Open Door") brought in foreign companies and products beginning in the mid-1970s. The policy eased restrictions on entrepreneurial economic activity while reducing forms of protection and social welfare for the vast majority of Egyptians. Under President Hosni Mubarak, who came to power after Sadat's assassination in 1980, the momentum has increased, and the social transformations and pressures have been enormous. There is a widespread sense among Egyptians now that individualism and opportunism are newly hegemonic, and attitudes toward new wealth are summed up in the nickname given to a certain popular model of Mercedes-Benz, the khanzira, hog, which of course is an unclean animal for Muslims. The mayor in another story, "Arabi," is driven in the same model car.

"Cold?" he asked. He seemed surprised. She tugged at the edges of her blouse collar.

"Freezing!"

He punched a button next to a small cassette player and the warmth began slowly to take effect. She eased back. He pushed another button and all the car windows closed.

"I love the cold, d'you?" he shouted, whipping the steering wheel around.

"I love warmth and good company."

Trees and houses flashed by. She saw neon lights reflected in the windshield.

The warmth teased at her roving thoughts, making her forget the hole in her stocking that she'd tried to hide with the hem of her dress, and her big toe, which had almost a clear view from the tip of her dilapidated shoe, and her recurring disgust at the paltriness of her salary that didn't stretch, and wouldn't stretch, to buying a winter coat. She thanked her Lord for the coincidence that had brought her together with this long-ago friend on such a bitterly cold night. He might never have noticed her despite the few feet his car had been from the entrance to the government bureau where she worked. He might never have invited her, treating her to a free ride home.

His voice pulled her from her thoughts.

"Hey, where'd you go?"

She took a deep breath. "Out into the world."

Smiling, he bent his face toward her. "The world, sweetheart—it's just a question of balls."

Surprise caught her tongue. His features seemed changed somehow, almost as if she had never seen him before. Her memory went back to its tangled thoughts and images. They were son and daughter of the same neighborhood in the same small coastal city, but she hadn't seen him for years. She'd heard that he had left for faraway places.

She studied the contours of his face, encased now in rough wrinkles. He was graying around the temples, too, even though he wasn't beyond his forties. His shirt-collar was starched, true, but his necktie seemed too startlingly red. It didn't go with his checked wool vest.

They were almost to the neighborhood whose main street had once embraced them both. He cut off the motor. If only all places of work could be obliterated and all overtime cancelled on cold winter nights, and if only she didn't have to leave the warmth of the car.

"It's all ice out there," she said, her voice hoarse. He turned the steering wheel. "Let's ride around for a bit," he said too loudly for the small space of the car. "After all, we're having a chat, aren't we? You know, life's a story of lucky moments."

He turned at the intersection just past their street. To regain the main thoroughfare, he circled the market and passed the bus stop that now looked like a pile of scrap metal. He took out a pack of cigarettes, fancy ones, and tried to give her one. She refused it by saying her chest hurt.

He paid no attention to what she said. He pressed the button on the gold lighter and the space between their faces was suddenly bright. She noticed how puffy his eyelids were, and how dull his gaze.

The tumult and noise rose as he worked the cassette player. He glanced surreptitiously at her legs and she hurriedly pressed them together.

His voice shot out with the smoke rings.

"What d'ya think of that singer?"

"It's not a bad voice, but I can't understand a thing."

He moved his head in time to the music, echoing it.

"Do you know, I bought the tape and the cassette player and on top of that this hog, plus an import-export office and two buildings for a million pounds cash—that's right, by god, a million."

His chest puffed out.

"That's god's truth, a full million—in cash."

"And the guy who owns that voice," he added after a moment, "I could buy him all for myself too and for whatever price he names." His syllables strutted by her with the cockiness of a man sure of his stature in the world.

Her eyes circled narrowly in the restricted space of the car. She bit her fingernails and tried to squeeze out of the uncomfortable intimacy of the moment with a sudden loud question.

"Do you remember when we used to jump from the wall of the school, giving our bags and clothes to Fahima's son, Bassa, so he'd have to carry them? Then we'd run and run until we reached the shore, and my mother would smell the salt on my body and get my father to spank me!"

He frowned, rubbed his head as if trying to regain a memory. "And when we used to go to the Foreigners' Quarter," she went on. "Remember that? We'd scramble after the buses and hang on, and we made bets on who would find the most tin cans in the trash."

The brake swallowed her laugh and her head almost hit the windshield.

His face grew dark and his features seemed to sharpen.

"Enough now, let's go back," he said.

When the smell of rot surged through the car abruptly, she knew they were close to the neighborhood, to the street that had once united them.

She broke the silence. "I'll make a bet with you."

The motionless contours of his face were imprinted on the window. "A bet on what?"

"Stand outside for an hour at the bus station, by yourself— didn't you say you like the cold?"

He turned his face toward her in amazement. "Is that much of a challenge?"

"So you'll do it?"

"Starting tomorrow."

She pointed to an old house at the end of the market street.

"Let me out over there." She slammed the door shut and went around the car toward his door as he began to move the steering wheel.

She looked him in the eye.

"If I win the bet, I get the car."

The frost dug its claws into her hunched body, and the distance between her waiting and a long line of barely distinguishable cars was an interminable stretch of ice.

"Al-Murahana"
December 1988
Dunya saghira, pp. 73-80

February

In Egypt today, a growing number of women and girls are practicing the new veiling. They have a variety of reasons to do so, and a range of practices from which to choose, from a simple scarf over the hair to a more enveloping cloak that covers the hair and upper body, or to niqab, *a further step adopted by a small minority of "veiled" women, which entails covering the entire face except for the eyes and wearing gloves.*

"Some might think they can hide behind heavy cloth, but nothing in the end can veil the emotions. Feelings are the human condition, and it is natural to express and practice them, whether one covers one's head or not. We must free ourselves from sources and symbols of over-bearing power and authority, even if they are mere bits of cloth."

The sea's touch did not pacify her. She slipped off her shoes and poked them under her arm. The smell of iodine doused her. The screaming of the waves forced itself into her waking mind. Her unbound hair floated away from her and toward the sails atop those distant boats, while the wind toyed with her dress, lifting it to sit meekly beneath. Her bare feet crunched oyster shells and conches that lay flung across the sand.

"You never listen! Here—take it."

She clamped the thermometer between the girl's lips.

"Going down to the sea in February! You're an idiot, young lady!" The loud anger in that bellow expelled an acrid breath full into her face.

She opened one eye, just halfway. She saw her mother's bloated face, mirroring the fleshy body, the rolls of fat that jiggled every time she sputtered her words of reproach.

She tossed her shoes some distance and waded in. The child-like caress of the water's surface tickled her legs. She angled her head toward the sky that had no end and noticed the murky wetness gathering deep inside the clouds as the dark seagull shapes circled overhead.

Drops pelted her forehead. She stretched out her tongue as far as she could to catch the cold pellets of water. She invited the rain to come along. Lifting the two of them, the waves hurled both her and the rain, her companion, straight into the heart of the blue expanse. Cold and refreshed, she and the rain rose once more with the leaping wave, their delirium washed by salt and the fragrance of iodine.

One day as she was changing her clothes, her aunt had caught sight of her. Her own bosom falling in a sigh, the aunt gazed steadily at her breasts.

"The lupine beans have grown into green apples, and by tomorrow they'll be giving way to pomegranates."

When the aunt's eyes traveled lower, she hid her small nest, a laugh slipping from her pensive, half-closed eyes.

The squat houses on the beach were sheeted in silence and solitude. She ran barefoot, her clothes sticking to her simmering body, her cough getting ahead of her every few minutes.

Her mother gave the thermometer a hard shake and smacked her lips loudly in dismay. "Now take us, for instance. Any one of us. We didn't dare even look out the window without getting permission first."

She settled another blanket over her warm daughter.

"You must sweat!" She turned to the door and switched off the light.

"I'll bring you some lemon drink."

Eyeing her mother's shadow as it moved beyond the door, still partly open, she tightened the covers over her chest and brought them up to her chin.

"Mama," she whispered. "I know my temperature will go up, I know the cough won't stop now. But it's just like last time, it's only a cold, and it will go away. Why would it be so awful, though, for you to take off that heavy thing hiding your hair, which is so pretty? Why can't you take off that thick cloth that jails your body and come down to the sea?

"I've never seen you go down to the shore, summer or winter, mama. If you would come once, just one time, mama, you'd fall in love with it. Like I have. Even in the middle of February."

"Fabrayir"
Cairo,1995
Ibda', 13 no. 4 (April 1996), pp. 79-80
Nakhb iktimal al-qamar, pp. 27-31

The Work Gang

"The balcony of my mother's home directly overlooked the court building. At any time of day or night, there were police vans full of prisoners arriving. Sometimes the prisoners were in chains, whether they were men, women, or children. I hate the sight of those vans. Since I have a long history of political activism, I know them well. To be in one is to be in a prison cell. It is especially hard when you see children in them, the sight of children's eyes peering through the bars. It does not matter what they have done. What matters is how they are treated."

Huddled on a bit of pavement, squeezing a small packet under her arm, she made herself as tiny as she could. She had the chill weather and a broken spirit to cloak her.

The soldier on duty eyed her doubtfully. Nearby, the fierce shrilling of a siren grew even louder. Her eyes flitted across the scene, unable to settle.

It was not yet dawn. The hiss of the wind in her heart warned of danger. The inky van pulled in. Where its sides merged with the roof she could see the tiny apertures crisscrossed by heavy wire. Behind them moved blurry shadows. A pair of soldiers stood on the van's rear steps. Gray faces, haggard stares.

The soft rapping on the front door roused her, the grief slumping permanently against her heart. She snatched up the old shawl lying there and snuggled it around her shoulders; she pushed the door open, only a crack. The pupils of her eyes narrowed. He was

about the same age, anyway. She moved toward him, her arms opening wide as the bleakness and the stink of rotting garbage slapped
her.

Soldiers were massing around the van as she ran toward it. A
raw hand shoved her away. The packet slid from her. Heavy boots
flattened it.

"Not allowed to stand here, ma'am. Move off."

She backed away, her eyes trained on the van's rear door as they
shuffled down, one on the heels of another. She saw shaved heads,
faces branded by the scoring of time, asphalt once ground into
their clothes. The tallest one looked not more than thirteen, if that.
Eyes once widened by innocent pleasures now were set hard in
aversion; deep cracks riddled bare, swollen feet. Iron chains circled
their wrists, binding each one to the next.

She saw a fleshy face, glazed eyes, a mouth partly hidden under
a dense moustache, a faded overcoat slung over a *gallabiyya*—for
he wore the traditional robe rather than a shirt and trousers. The
stubby, fleshy man shadowed those boy-men. He was clutching a
stick, a branch stripped of leaves, stinging their backs until their
heads sagged against their chests. The nearer his senior officer came,
the more ferocious grew the blows.

Whatever words might have come faded in her throat. Her
eyes strained to tell them apart, to make out features, faces. But it
was her feelings that pointed him out first. He lifted his head fur-
tively, his face seeming to lengthen and tighten even more. She saw
a protruding jawbone. She saw sunken eyes whispering harshness
and twitching in fear. Nothing else was left.

The soldiers were not allowing anyone to get by or even to
approach. She stood waiting a little apart from the station door
until the last soldier had gone in. Then she hurried inside and ran
to the nearest ticket window. Which train would carry the work
gang? Someone waved toward an outlying track. The two front

cars were for those workers, she heard, and the rest for ordinary passengers.

The furious thudding in her chest raced ahead of her tapping heels.

The blue windows were obstructing her vision. The doctor's burly hand struggled to pull out the thing that was tightening its hold on the tiny world inside its mama's belly, taking cover from the bullets, the dry bread, the screaming of children, and its mother's cold mattress. As if it knew that its father had strayed far and would not return, as if it knew that its birth was war.

The boys squatted on the station platform, hunched over themselves, chained hands hanging between their knees, eyes to the ground. She breathed the smell of him. She moved nearer. The soldier tried to block her but she did not move. When he shoved her she screamed.

"Get your hand off me you bas—"

Her shout brought over the officer in charge. He looked at her parched face, the bruised eyes. He turned his head away. "Leave her alone, man!" His bark froze the soldier in place. A shaking hand saluted. "At your command, sir."

The officer's eyes came back to her.

"Your boy?"

She nodded, her eyes traveling with the whistle of the train.

"Attention!" he bellowed at the soldiers.

They fell into line. The boys got to their feet. The short man shook his stripped branch at them until they sorted themselves out, a linked chain facing the steps into the train. The youngster squinted in her direction. The teardrops floating on those eyes spoke words held back. Rebukes, shyness, shame.

39

The station clock struck the hour. Wheels rolled and the whistle pierced the air. She thrust herself forward toward the itinerants' car, but the soldiers kept her from climbing on. She cried out.

"You can get to him from over there," said someone. The screech of the wheels grew deafening. She ran as fast as she could and just barely caught the last train car. A passenger's tough grip yanked her inside. She pushed through the packed car. Maybe she would find a bit of floor where she could collect her confused thoughts. She stood staring through the window at the ground. Her eyes tried to move beyond the rails and the wounded years, as her heart uncoupled itself and pitched away, pitched toward the car where the work gang huddled.

"Al-Tarhila"
November 1993
Al-Thaqafa al-jadida, no. 66, March 1994, pp. 46-47
Nakhb iktimal al-qamar, pp. 7-12

Palm Trees and the Sea

"There was a poet from Asyut, from Upper Egypt where my father's family comes from. I met him at a poetry conference, where he recited a poem in honor of the Palestinian poet Mahmud Darwish. He was young. But because he had had the education of a shaykh, *a religious scholar, he wore a robe and turban. His poetry was bold. We became friends, and sometime later he mailed a letter from Asyut, from the desert rises, to me in Port Saïd, on the sea. 'I'm coming to visit you. Make me some of that fish and rice that you talk about.' I waited. A day, a week, a month. Then I learned that he had died, not yet aged forty. I learned of his death by reading the newspaper. I saw the announcement of the* ta'bin, *the ceremony of mourning that occurs forty days after the death. And I wrote the story."*

Shaykh *in this story plays on the double (and related) meaning of the term: as a scholar and therefore source of learning and authority; and as an elderly, perhaps venerable, man. In Egyptian colloquial Arabic,* shaykh *is also used teasingly or sarcastically.*

The epithet of "poet-stallion" is appropriate to a shaykh, *for it is a traditional Arabic figure for poetic inspiration. Further down in the paragraph the writer exploits the potential ambiguity between the words* shi'r *(poetry) and* sha'r *(hair), which appear identical in print because short vowels are not ordinarily printed in Arabic text.*

The customary way to serve hot tea in Egypt is in a thick, clear glass, although now teacups have become a sign of sophistication for some.

"The son of death." That was what they called him. "There is an instant for death," I said, "and age upon age for the truth."

Wounds to the heart; and with the wind of the mountains you come to me, to the innermost waters. The gulls light on your chest and you summon the little fish: "I'm dying for ocean perch with rice, popping over the flame."

I can see how the fish of the unwise cities have swallowed you.

The sea pulls voyagers to where the palms and mountains lie, and the heartbeat flares in death's bosom. The dream was as sweeping as the flood in your eyes; in laughing scorn you toyed with the turban wrapping your head.

"Well now, time to leave."

"There's still time, our master the *shaykh*. I'll make you a glass of tea."

He laughed and his boyish eyes glistened.

"How can you be a *shaykh* when you're not yet forty?" I pestered.

"Daughter of the sea! You don't know what goes on in the hollows of the mountains. I lived inside, there in the mountains, with my little brothers. The cane of the Qur'an school's *shaykh* stung us, as we sat in rows on the floor. Our small backs were inflamed in the coldest of months. Trying to memorize the Holy Book's sacred verses, we opened our mouths, we repeated and repeated, for that was all we were to learn. The mountains' echoes answered, for we had only the mountains as playmates. The scorching sun, frost on our fingers and toes—that was all we had. I hadn't yet spoken my dream when they set the turban on my head. The poet-stallion had visited me in secret, across the mountains, and it ferried me on and on, constantly moving, from the land of God to the folk of God, always moving, from place to place, from folk to folk. Until I met you, daughter of the waters, and I saw how your volcano of hair exploded across the flesh of the waves."

"Those lines of yours make me think of the trees holding fast in the face of the wind, of the truth probing the sun's core."

"Children of the waters, you always go too far. But the witness is God's. Fresh perch with rice is the sweetest thing there is."

"No one can outdo you when you speak," I said, busy with the tea. "Believe me, I always give you your due. Because I hold you so dear, I'm that afraid for you."

He looked straight at me, his own face brimming. His spirit towered like the mountains and was as gentle and fragile as the eye of a child. And the bridge between us was built of letters plaited from the palm trees and the sea.

"Al-Nakhil wa'l-bahr"
July 1988
Dunya saghira, pp. 49-53

Shadow Puppets

"I don't know why, but I feel very close to the elderly. It is especially painful to me when I see them unable to enjoy or practice life. Sometimes an affection that goes back many years is simply not enough."

The woman's husband is Abu'l-Sayyid, "father of al-Sayyid." Parents are customarily called by the name of their eldest child or eldest son. [Al-]Sayyid is a given name, but it also echoes a polite term of male address: "the mister," and the term by which direct descendants of the Prophet Muhammad are called.

She made her nightly rounds through the apartment. She turned out the light in the bathroom and made her way into the living room. The glare from the light bored into her. She slumped against the wall, pressing the light-switch button off with a flattened palm.

Only the outside door was left now. No, it wasn't locked; she hadn't expected it to be. In the kitchen she gathered up the debris ringing the garbage can. She bent over slowly and hoisted the can, one hand on the bottom, the other on the rim. She set it down next to the neighbors' garbage outside on the back stairway.

"Karima! Karima."

Her step slowed. She turned to face the wall opposite the new neighbors' bedroom window.

On more than one night she'd paused, waited, swung around to look. It felt like someone was spying on her as she watched the shadows moving along the wall. She held her breath, just for seconds.

There they were, bending toward each other, blending into one. She rubbed herself against the wall until she felt a shiver pass through her sagging body. She took a couple of steps back, raising her lined face. Her big, round, keen eyes staring at the wall held the shadows of an elapsed beauty mingled with the *kohl* of the years, the eyeliner she had once worn. The traces of the face he had loved were still there, even if her hair did look more like strands of ice now.

Breathing fast, she caught the reverberations of laughter splashed across the wall. She stepped nearer. The elongated fingertips on the wall were undoing pajama buttons. His hands nudged the straps of a nightgown. Breasts peeping out, hair ebbing, flowing, lips touching, hands locking, a pair of legs rising, falling.

"Karima! Karima."

The reedy voice roused her, its thread broken by a fitful cough. Guiding herself with her hands running along the wall, she padded toward the one light that remained on, a strip of yellow seeping under the bedroom door. She turned the doorknob softly and opened the door just a little. His back braced against the bed frame, Abu'l-Sayyid was waiting for her. It was a boxy room, made more cramped by its contents: an old-fashioned wardrobe missing one panel; an oval table accommodating bottles of medicine, a set of dentures, cod-liver oil, a dirty spoon, and an overturned bowl; a chair by the bed; and a dusty radio minus dials and buttons. The picture on the wall hung lopsided, its glass fractured: a crew of sailors on the deck of a ship.

Her foot struck a crutch lying on the floor alongside the bed. When he reached out, she put her open hand in his and sat down next to him on the bed without a word.

"Where'd, uh, you go, Karima?" Through his stammer she could make out a strain of reproof.

"No, nowhere—I was... in the bathroom," she replied, her voice unsteady.

She saw the tired sadness in his eyes. He dropped his head, silent.

The sound of the steamships ... louder, nearer. So many sounds she could confuse, but not the steamships' voices, for they always punctured her heart before they could reach her ear. Those days when she would wait for Abu'l-Sayyid, who was always going away; and then, those days when she would wait for al-Sayyid, who had grown up and gone to sea, leaving behind him a hollowness the size of the world.

Then Abu'l-Sayyid would tease her. "The son of a duck is a swimmer!" She would laugh and her thoughts would travel.

The growling of the dogs broke the silence in the street. She got to her feet, wanting to look out of the window: three male dogs, chasing a female, fighting until the strongest triumphed and jumped on her, and stayed, pressing close upon her. She followed them, her eyes wandering across the window, her lips moist, until her neighbor—the one on the ground floor—threw a rock and the dogs scattered.

She closed the window and sat down once again next to Abu'l-Sayyid as he watched her, saying nothing. She inspected his frail, angular body, her stare shifting from the top of his head—the few thin strands of white hair combed carefully straight back—and his pinched, blankly wandering eyes, shrouded in rough wrinkles, to his bumpy chest and his legs, one of them useless ever since a long-ago venture out to sea.

The yellow light in the room fell cruelly on her eyes.

She moved closer to Abu'l-Sayyid, close enough to smell the sea salt in his sweat. Without warning she felt overcome by the numbness of that very first night: a mild pain, a newborn ecstasy, and the sea poured its waves through her, rising, falling, rising and then falling, plunging to her heart. When she came back to her senses, the pain had gone and all was still.

She stretched out next to Abu'l-Sayyid, whose cough had quieted. He leaned toward her and his skinny, feeble hand dabbed at her head. He wrapped his arm around her waist, pulling them closer together.

Her fingertips touched each white hair on his head. Her hand crept from his chest to the rise of his belly, and then on, dropping into emptiness.

She tried to get up. But he pressed his open palms against her shoulders. "Wait, stay, maybe..." The words were muffled, hard to make out.

She slipped from between his hands gently. Her voice was so low that he could barely hear as she looked at the figures that had begun to move on the wall.

"I'll turn off the lamp. This light is too bright. It hurts my eyes."

"Khayal al-zill"
Port Saïd, 1986
Al-Nawras, pp. 17-22

Tea Grown Cold

"I love the night. I don't sleep. I write most of my stories at night. Perhaps it is because I do not hold traditional jobs. Working in the theater as a producer, I work at night. Everything happens at night."

Maybe her heart would shrivel from grief, but the night would forever be her great love. She filled the kettle, put it on the flame, and moved away softly toward the balcony. She was in love with late nights and song, with dancing and the rain.

She wished the night a good evening. It made no response.

The moon disappeared behind the high rooftops.

"What's the matter, dear night?" she asked. "Why so silent? Only yesterday you were my companion, my friend of summer and winter, of the stirrings of youth... oh dear, it looks like I've forgotten the tea, doesn't it? I'm sorry."

She poured a full glass of tea, picked out her prettiest tray, and set it on the low balcony wall.

She made ready a seat for him. She called him. She adjured him by the Almighty to speak, but no answer came.

Was he tired of her? Was he bored? She whispered the questions. As ready to leave as the years that had slipped from her life? Or maybe, creeping behind the raucous evenings, he had forgotten her? She summoned him to a glass of hot tea, a perfect one from her own hand. His stare needled her: glowing coals of neon trained upon her. He let out a sickly, high-pitched laugh, shaking the towering buildings gorged with their cement-block graves. Light trucks and vans flipped over. The screaming vanished into the howling of the dogs, the indistinct voices.

She studied his empty place. This was not her nighttime—not her passion from which wafted the smell of old houses. Not her night, that lightly fondled the laughing balconies, patting those streets with a gentle hand that they might sleep in peace. Wakeful and watchful would he stay, with the tiny new shoes bought for the Ramadan feast day that waited, peeking from under the bed. And he would drink in her sadness.

She dreamed the return of the beloved night and she waited.

She sang and the echo came back in stone. The tea grew cold.

"Shay barid"
Cairo, 1994
Published as "Hafat al-shurfa"
with three other stories under the rubric "Shay barid,"
Majallat al-Katiba, no. 7, June-July 1994, pp. 34-35.
Published as "Shay barid," *Nakhb iktimal al-qamar,* pp. 33-36.

A Toast to the Full Moon

"A desire to live must come from inside. And he wanted to go on living, in death, according to his own way of life. The story assaults ideas about the supernatural, beliefs in the concept of fate and so on. And you know, the ancient Egyptians believed in another life inside death, and inside the tomb itself. Not only is the tomb sacred; it represents life as much as it does death. Inside the pyramids there were perfectly engineered holes to let the sun in. There were beds, drinking vessels, jewelry. I don't know how, but Egyptians have always had a fierce desire for life despite all the hardship. That is still the way it is."

In medieval Cairo, families built tombs with enclosed courtyards so they could go on holidays and spend time with their dear departed ones. The City of the Dead, on the edge of the city of the living, is now encircled by new dwellings, by high rises. Life and death mingle. At the same time, spending time and resources on elaborate mourning has been a practice that reformers from the late nineteenth century on have attacked as a waste of national resources and as contrary to Islam's emphasis on simple piety and the basics of the faith. Mentioned here also is another traditional practice—with no basis in Islam—that more recent social activists have tried to eradicate, female genital mutilation (FGM)—sometimes called "female circumcision" and practiced in parts of Africa.

"And, that night, it is as if the moon was sipping beer with us."

"I told my uncle—the one who still lives in our village—that I need a tomb four meters square. 'One with a staircase,' I said, 'so you can go right down inside, and a cushion to rest my skull on.'" He swallowed the last bit of tea and shook his finger as he addressed the young woman.

"When you come to see me, make sure you bring stuffed grape leaves, the ones you make yourself. Understand?"

She nodded, smiling.

"Right, pal," said their friend. "So you can just take it as easy as you want."

"You think you're so smart—all right then, you just wait until it's all decked out in red brick." He fell back against his chair as he spoke. "The gravedigger wouldn't even dig it for me. He says foolishness like this is against the law."

Their friend rubbed his head, ruffling his hair. "If you close it in completely, it will make you miserable. Give yourself a window, or else the heat will scorch you and make your life hellfire."

He shook his head. "Who cares? It doesn't matter what shape I'm in once I'm in the fire."

She looked at his babylike face, at his sunken eyes behind the glasses and his tenth cigarette.

She stood up abruptly. "Excuse me, I'm going to the bathroom."

She left the two of them sitting there. Alone behind the door, she let the tears come.

She knew the doctor had warned him against staying up late, against cigarettes, against any excitement whatsoever. He knew perfectly well that his heart would not survive another operation. Doing what he'd been told not to do, he would say to her, "God forgives all sins." And then he would whisper, his mouth next to her ear, "I love life as much as you love the sea."

As soon as she stepped outside the bathroom, she could hear their chuckles. She went over to the table. The moon was full. He twisted to face her. She rested her palm on his shoulder, and gently he patted her hand. From a recess of the garden, she caught a whiff of the shrubby trees that ringed them. His eyes smiled, untroubled.

"Look here, brother, look how pretty this girl is—now there's Egyptian beauty for you." A feathery shiver brushed her heart. She sat down close to him. He studied her.

"You know, you look just like my daughter -"

"You have a daughter, and you hide her from me?" their friend interrupted.

He snorted. "She's ten years old, see. You could be—pardon me—her grampa. Have some shame, man."

He withdrew his hand from hers and raised his head to meet the sky that had uncoiled itself before them on that moonlit night. Salty water massed in his eyes.

"You know, the day my friend died, the one who kept on about how women should get the same amount of inheritance as men and how girls shouldn't have their private parts cut off, my little girl drew a picture of the Pyramids, all in black. The sun was the color of blood and there wasn't a single wave on the water."

His voice was scratchy. "She loved him so much, you know. He used to tell her stories. All the time, telling her stories."

Silence closed in on their evening palaver. As always he hastened to break it.

"I tell you what, let's stay up all night, what do you think? Let's drink to the full moon."

Their friend shook himself. His baldness gleamed in the moon's glow. "Now *shaykh*, really! D'you have enough breath?" He slapped his hand against his forehead and looked at his watch. "Hey, that reminds me—the doctor's appointment."

She started out of her seat, calling loudly as she rose. "I'm coming with you."

His kindly eyes quieted her.

"Believe me, it's not worth all of this. He's just going to put a bit of metal in my gut and check my blood pressure, and he'll tell me I have to get a blood test and X-ray. *Shaykha*, don't make such a fuss."

She stared at the bushes rippling in the corner of the garden. The third one of them interrupted her straying thoughts as the object of their concern lit another cigarette.

"Come on, fellow, go easy on yourself, your heart isn't well."

"Pipe down, you geezer," he teased back.

Her eyes moved from one to the other and she smiled.

"The heart that's not well is the one that doesn't know love. We'll stay up, we'll talk, we'll laugh. We'll keep living. We will toast the full moon."

"Nakhb iktimal al-qamar"
Cairo, 1996
Al-Ahram, 1996
Published in Salem's collection by the same name, pp. 17-22.

Cusp

"Suspended moments. If they last too long, it is so easy to lose one's way."

- 1 -

Time moves on in a monotone
The cries make their circuit
The edges of the seats are worn away
Suitcases block the passage
And the ancient driver shifts the wheel slowly above the filthy, rust-hewn tires.

- 2 -

With one feeble hand
She moved the soiled curtains aside
Her faded eyes glued themselves to the windowpane
His face came to her, reproachful
Wiping away patches of the dust of times gone by
"Please don't shut your door."

- 3 -

She curled into her seat
Alone and far above her wound

Their final supper together
Seesawing between the bells' tolling and passion's minaret
Time passes, and passes,
And the ancient driver—still and the same—turns the wheel.

- 4 -

A moment remaining
between
the onward rush of the car toward nowhere
and her cold mattress on the rim of the night.

"Tarawuh"
Ibda' (February 1998), p. 62
Al-Thaqafa al-jadida, no. 114 (March 1998), p. 105

Bags of Candy

"I wrote this the night Farag Fouda, prominent thinker on Islam and society, was assassinated by Islamists. That happened in 1992, after Fouda's critical comments on 'the Islamic tendency,' which the Egyptian press published, had grown sharper and more frequent. After hearing the news, I could not sleep; and I wrote the story at dawn. Why was it this particular memory of my childhood that came to me that night?

"I grew up in Hayy al-Zahir, an area of Cairo known as a neighborhood of minorities. In our building our neighbor was Coptic, there was a Greek family and an Armenian family, and on the ground floor there was a Jewish family. Rachel—she was a seamstress. We all loved each other and visited, and we exchanged gifts on each other's holidays. We did not feel sensitivities about religion. We all knew that we belonged to God and the nation.

"It was a bit different at the nuns' school, though. There was a certain harshness about the religion. And imposing authority on children in the name of a religion is confusing to them. What happens to their innocence? I remember memorizing some of the Christian rituals. My father punished me."

Fatima, name of the Prophet Muhammad's most celebrated daughter, is one of the names most identified with Islam that a female can have.

H e waited just until his wife had finished arranging the entry hall. He made his way along the line of chairs.

"Where's Fatima?" he asked.

She was picking up a scrap of paper from the floor and she did not bother to straighten up. "What do you want her for?" she called out.

"I got a letter from the school."

"May God not bring us evil! Any news we don't want to hear?"

"No, not in the letter. But they want me first thing tomorrow morning in the headmistress's office. Where's your daughter, woman?"

"You'll find her over there, over toward where you're standing." She jerked her head in the direction of the balcony. His eyes picked out the girl. She was squatting in a recess of the balcony, mumbling and humming something to herself. The bristly hedge that overhung the balcony wall reared above her.

He went over to her. She stopped murmuring and he stepped closer.

"Hey, what are you saying, there?"

She stood up, alert. "Nothing, Father, nothing at all."

Her back was plastered against the hedge-topped wall and her eyes rolled away from his shadow, a silhouette that sat implacably on her chest.

He repeated his question. "What are those words you keep on saying?"

She held her breath.

His patience was gone. "I said, what are you saying to yourself," he shouted.

The strains of the piano cascaded from the East Hall to play with her tiny spirit, bearing it high, as far as she could see into the circling distances.

The dirt of the courtyard choked her little shoes as she stood waiting her turn to be called. The teacher, a squat figure wrapped in a nun's habit, held her cane in a tight hand as she separated the girls going into one of the chilly, badly-lit schoolrooms from the girls who were entering the East Hall that gave onto the courtyard.

On Sundays, time passed so dully. She perched motionless on a wooden bench as dusty as her shoes, in that cold room, until the bell would announce that it was time to go.

Once she had slipped into the East Hall. She had seen little butterflies dancing around the piano by candlelight and a man cloaked entirely in black whose beard seemed to reach all the way down to his paunch. A fancy crown-like thing sat on his head, and his chest revealed the priestly silver and gold chains that flashed as he moved. A sheaf of colored sacks dangled from one fist.

She stood with the other girls, chanting whatever words they were, the ones that would fetch the sacks of candy and the bread rounds dotted with sesame seeds.

"What's your name?" barked the teacher, her cane touching the little one's forehead.

Her memory redeemed her. "Theresa." She thought of the daughter of her Armenian neighbor, who would play with her in the empty, unpaved, open space at the center of the building. She found herself being led behind the piano's chords into the eastern half of the courtyard.

She awakened to her father's voice. He was shaking her, hard. "Speak up!"

She shivered and stammered out a few of the words she had chanted. He shoved his hands into her armpits and dragged her inside. Pieces of candy scattered across the ground as the sound of a man bellowing filled all the space there was.

At the sound of his shouting the mother sped over and threw her arms around her daughter. The little one shrank into her mother's quivering chest, shoving her head as far in to that softness as she could. The voice of the piano merged with the voice of the father.

"Where's the belt?"

"Akyas al-hilwa"
Cairo, 1991
Al-Thaqafa al-jadida no. 55 (April 1993), p. 83
Nakhb iktimal al-qamar, pp. 37-41

Rage

"I had been visiting my husband in Tura prison. It was 1985. The prison is south of Cairo, south of Helwan. You have to walk a long way to reach it, and it sits against a desert mountain. You can see people climbing that mountain, chained together, work gangs on their way to toil. It is an inhuman sight, and if you are visiting a political prisoner they try to keep you waiting until the gangs are gone. I returned exhausted to downtown Cairo. There is an old church there, across from the old Journalists' Syndicate building, and the bell reminds me of the church bell we could always hear in my neighborhood when I was growing up. I looked at the wall around the church. It was very high. It reminded me of the prison wall. I went into the Journalists' Syndicate and wrote this story."

- 1 -

The wall looms high now, and forever, its tongue loose and fluent. The bell is ringing as it always has on Sunday mornings. Nuns scurry across the open courtyard. The father blesses them once they have performed the kissing of the hand.

The wall stands between you and me.

With both hands I pounded, but I was sore and tired. The guards pushed me away. I searched for a hammer.

Lower your face, you said. Kiss the hand of our father. You are still little: he will grant you his blessing. Kneel and ask forgiveness, for you have lagged behind. Cast the evil spirits from your heart.

61

The ground is cold. My dress does not even cover my knees. The church courtyard is a desert that reaches on and on.

- 2 -

The officers wrenched you from the bosom of warmth in the deep of the night. Nothing was left but the fragrance of books and intimacy. When they made their move to pull you away, you clung to the earth. The wall is ever planted there, mute as death.

The slaps come and go. I cache myself inside my fear. I hold my bladder. That hand still reaches for me even if it is arrested halfway, waiting. Inside me a voice murmurs.

"I've been neglectful, my father, neglectful." In asking your blessing, my mind adds. But you know I do not like to kneel.

- 3 -

I aimed the hammer at the wall's heart and soul. I battered it with all the strength I had. The horizon stretched long before me, color upon color, and the breezes carved out flowers and children on the river's brow.

The eye of the sun laughed and the breath of life, so sad and forlorn, quit its retirement. Young now, the breath of life stretched forth, expanding, waiting, until the bell would quit knelling.

"Al-Ghadab,"
finished in Port Saïd, 1985.
Al-Nawras, pp. 9-11
Also in Idwar al-Kharrat, *al-Kitaba 'abra al-naw'iyya*
(Cairo: Dar Sharqiyyat, 1994), p. 119.

My Friend "Patriot"

"In the part of Giza where I lived for awhile there was an old fruit seller. When Infitah *came, he turned his fruit stand into an* Atari *shop. Kids would pay twenty-five* piasters *to play. I would watch them from my window, playing this video game that resembled war, and imagine the rockets coming off the screen.*

"The Gulf War was a war of big organizations. It had nothing to do with people. Even the military commentator sounded like a parrot. But no game can rescue the poor from war. And no war game rescues them from the odor of things that have rotted."

With the single word "Patriot," Salem puts before us a layered world of the local and the global, of desire and oppression. Not only superpower missiles that are seen to fulfill superpower goals carry the label of "Patriot"—so do consumer goods, smilingly offered by a European-looking model on television, or menacingly by an American superhero, invading so many homes, even the narrator's dilapidated rented room. Global politics, the economy of the street where entertainment and consumption reign, and a fragile national infrastructure all shape each other. Though this story was written more than a decade ago, readers might find new insights about Egyptian popular (as opposed to official) feelings about the Gulf War and about events since then. What, after all, should the word "patriot" mean? And what does the invasion of the English word, rather than use of its Arabic counterpart, mean to our contemporary world? Meanwhile, what reality does the "virtual" carry?

This story was first published while the Gulf War was still going on. For several months afterward, whenever Ibtihal went into a popu-

lar downtown cafe that writers frequent, Zahrat al-Bustan, *someone would call out,* Ahlan, ya Batriyut! (*Welcome, Patriot!*)

The smoke was beginning to overwhelm the room; it was stifling. I opened the window. But I couldn't bear the stings of the cold or the smell of decay coming from the light shafts that ran through the center of the building.

No one came to visit me in my room—or "my cell," as my one and only friend had named it, she who had gone away and not returned. An ash-gray mantilla was the only partition that separated the old wooden door from the corridor into the single room that huddled in the dubious embrace of those light shafts. Seeing its yellowish walls creep toward me from the edge of death simply made my depression worse. It was those walls that left me curled up into a ball: a still, silent lump on a narrow strip of light in the space between the chair and the desk.

From the corner of the room where the dull brown television sits, "Patriot" came to call. Whenever the picture dizzied my eyes, I'd climb up to the roof to fix the aerial so that this new fellow, this "Patriot," would not slip away—this "Patriot" who shared my room (or my cell). "Patriot"—I was waking up to this word, and falling asleep to it, too.

"The allied forces have launched sixty thousand missiles and conducted seven thousand raids. The aggressor has fired rockets aimed at our positions. But our courageous 'Patriot' has blocked them all."

I recalled seeing this "Patriot" at old Badawi's, whose shop stood where the alley met the street. He had replaced his fruit with Atari. The neighborhood's preschoolers and the pupils escaping from school used to gather there, as did some older youths and the elderly neighbors.

"To give your wash more whiteness, use 'Patriot'," the blonde miss announced loudly, holding up a blindingly white sheet. Was this detergent another "Patriot," or the same "Patriot" I saw on my screen?

Yes, I'd seen "Patriot" in old Badawi's shop, but I didn't know then that a missile would appear in my room or that its name would be "Patriot" too.

My gaze settled on the column of ants creeping along the window frame as the young blonde woman laughed again, with a wink. "To get rid of the smell of perspiration, to have a soft skin, use 'Patriot' brand soap. 'Patriot': always the best." Meanwhile, the news commentator, that smile stuck on his face, was insisting that the rocket launched by the aggressor the night before had caused neither casualties nor damage.

My brain dismissed the notion that this "aggressor" could be "Patriot." After all, he was just playing a delightful, on-screen game. It was the same game that my little inner voice had always told me to play. I used to sneak looks at the street, and into the shop, checking on how often the rockets were managing to block an attack. Whenever it happened the children would clap and argue over how many explosions there had been.

A huge, swaggering cockroach wearing a Superman outfit and carrying a spear in one hand shouts into the mass of cockroaches around him, "No force is mightier than ours!" just as a container of "Patriot" insect killer blasts unexpectedly and kills them instantly.

The cats' skirmishing grows louder, their meows drowning out the commentator's voice. They say it is mating season. The battle between the cats knocks over the garbage cans and the blows thud louder against the mute doors.

The few bits of furniture in my home now are rattling, popping over the flame of the smoke coming from the screen. The walls are swaying with the sounds of explosions that seem near enough to fall on my head.

Now the reception grows wavy again, this stupid box is useless! I'll throw it out the minute I move out of this room (and this cell).

The picture is still wavy, but I listen to the voice: "We've just received the following statement: A cat has given birth to three kittens. The owner has named one of them 'Great Patriot.'"

"Maybe the new kitten, Patriot, can stall this procession of cats," I told myself, as the electricity went out. It usually does this time of night. But, one of these days I will slide down those light shafts and no one will be able to catch me, not even "Patriot." After all, I didn't notice any of the missiles in the Atari game aiming at the light shafts.

A scratching sound rises from the corner of the room. Yes, the reception has come back. "The bombing continues," announces the ever-smiling commentator. "Our missiles have destroyed dams, bridges, and a factory that produces infant formula."

I pounded myself on the chest, sobbing. The reception was cut; voice and picture were no more.

I went right up to that stupid box. I shook it—no good. I switched channels. Nothing. I took off one shoe and hit the top of the box. As they say, "The goodhearted don't win."

I clenched my teeth. What was the use of this dumb "Patriot," if milk flowed uselessly with blood along the streets? "Patriot" turns away from the progress of the game, no longer wanting to see or to hear anything about it. I will banish it from my home.

I was suddenly very tired. I let out a long, loud sigh, keeping my eyes on this silenced box while my emptied-out self muttered to me. "Have the children finished their games? Did the cats bring the battle to new heights and has the milk vendor gone away? Will the rot that I smell rising from the shaft win out over all?"

"Sadiqi 'Batriyut'"
February 10, 1991
Dunya saghira, pp. 25-31

Little Things Don't Lie

"The moments when you are just drifting into sleep are moments of truthfulness with yourself. Of withdrawal and communion within. There are always things hidden under the covers that are terribly hard to say."

Evening came
As usual we dragged our heaviness to a bed carefully made up
The chilly walls are on watch
Eyes staring into black emptiness caught by surprise
And little things beneath the covers are concealed
"Fear, still fear"
Fatigue
Only a few betrayals
And a gentle understanding layer upon layer
Of a time past that will not return

I hid in a niche in my heart (it felt so natural by now), as the salt collected in a corner of my eye. I could see myself reflected in the mirror of the other world. Gazing at my metallic face turning, turning, I could see other faces, ones I know so well, revolving around mine. But their indistinct features were leading me astray. My watch.

My watch rolled off and splintered on a sheet of rusty iron. And little things. Little things peer outward—the tiny, well-sculpted crowns and tips, peering far, looking near: the thread that separates our bodies forever.

"Ashya' saghira la takdhibu"
1998
Al-Thaqafa al-jadida, no. 114 (March 1998), p. 105

Crumbs

"The young here are in crisis. They leave school with degrees but can find no work. Apartments are expensive and hard to find, and years go by with no hope of a stable place to live—indeed, without a stable life. They can barely pay for daily bread. I felt for this boy. His eyes were so intelligent. He did not realize that I could see him in the mirror inside the cafe. He did not know that I saw his humiliation. I went home and wrote."

He stood at a distance, off to the side under the hissing wooden radio, squinting at the chair now empty but for her quenched spirits.

He made a spindly figure, eaten away at the edges by squalor and drying skin, from his extremities to the drooping face whose expression he was powerless to change, sagging down to the dirty apron stretched across his belly.

The night was miserly, customers few. The words came out a sigh, expelling weary sorrow that lay in the very marrow of his bones.

As if trying to shake off his own shadow, he scurried toward a vacated table. He pressed a prematurely veiny and chapped hand against his threadbare rag, sweeping into a pile the scraps left by an old man who had just gone.

He was quite near now. She stopped playing with her food and looked up. It seemed to pounce on her, that gaze; to attack her in the guts of her exile. The eyes of her brother: nowhere. Her mother's face, crushed by so much waiting through the wintry nights.

Their silent breaths conversed, and argued. She pressed her jaws together and went back to toying with the cold contents of her plate.

She turned her back on the crackling of the radio and the irregular cough. She crossed the street, still damp from yesterday's rain. Under the pale light of the neon his shadow was visible, flicking among the tables and the crumbs of all those years.

"Futat"
Cairo 1996
Nakhb iktimal al-qamar, pp. 79-81

An Empty Tin Can

"Sometimes I have felt as though I'm in a state of siege—at work, at home, even in the street. Every so often they used to mount intensive observations. All of us—all of the political types—would be followed. This would go on for a month or two, and then it would ease off for a while. It was so obvious, and they were always pitiful people. I used to make them run. And it would just make me more determined to go on with political work and writing. But then the publishers—in cahoots with the authorities—would refuse my writing. You have to keep trying. It's what you'd call a vicious circle."

I spotted him—and his falcon's eyes—on the pavement that bisected the street. I shrugged off my suspicions and crossed, dodging traffic. His breathing behind me, amidst the throngs, choked my steps.

"The only way to deal with your qualms is to find out for certain," I told myself.

I swung inside the first bus that happened to come by. He overtook me and stuck to me like a barnacle. I swore to the ticket-taker that I'd meant to go a different route, and I jumped off at a traffic light. Before I could catch my breath, he was there, right behind me.

I made for him. He was in his late twenties. Everyday clothes, nothing remarkable. But I noticed a tiny instrument in the upper pocket of his shirt, something like a pen but not exactly.

71

"What do you want?" I screamed into his hawk's eyes.

"What do *you* want?" he sneered.

"If you don't go your own way, you'll be real, real sorry."

My hollering began to draw some of the passersby.

"I walk in the street whenever I feel like it, and however I want to, and I'll make you sorry you yelled at me." He was twisting and untwisting a metal chain around one index finger.

I balled my hand and jabbed at his chest.

"If I happen to notice you tailing me again, you can bet you'll taste your own hateful medicine!"

My shouting and my refusal to step back were attracting more and more people. His falcon eyes flicked across the place, and only a moment later he'd vanished into thin air.

I vomited the fury and resentment that congested me. The roiling in my chest was fiercer than the rays of the sun at the midday call to prayer. I cut into a side street. The tiny mosque perched there on the edge of the pavement was heaped with vacant shoes and stooped figures. I avoided them by taking a tunnel-like passageway that led to the building I wanted. My feet stumbled over an empty tin can. I kicked it as far as I could, following its bumpy progress along the hot asphalt.

I managed to catch the director in just before his usual time of departure. I apologized for being late and asked about several of my pieces that no doubt had been lodged in some drawer for months past. He pressed a button on his desk and spoke to someone in the next room. Minutes later the batch of papers lay before him.

Ice. My waiting, his silence.

"Sorry, it won't do." He pulled off his gold-framed glasses and stared into my fallen features. A wan smile crossed his face. His voice came quietly, cold.

"Unless we take out some paragraphs. Or redo the way the whole thing reads on the basis of our own expertise and experience."

I shot up from the chair as if suddenly bitten by some odious creature.

"I'd rather withdraw it," I said, holding out my hand.

He pushed his chair back.

"You're all like that, always in a hurry," he shouted, derisively now.

I was completely taken aback. "What do you mean by 'all'?"

The dark resentment that was congealing over his face seemed to stupefy him. I swallowed the sourness in my throat and walked out of his office, bruising the white pages in my grip.

When I reached my own little street, something seemed amiss. A line of women carrying heavy tin pots on their heads had descended on the waterpump at the end of the alley. In the adjacent dead-end lane I could make out alien faces and a black mound. I supported myself against the wall that led into my building, as I skirted carefully around the holes in the ground.

Batta and Sayyida, who had the ground floor, were standing at the entrance while little Ulaywa—Batta's son—romped nearby. I asked about the black mound. Sayyida hurried to speak.

"Baatia's son fell down the sewer pipe."

I climbed the stairs. My head spun with words of condolence for the boy's family and with the urgency of somehow finding two pounds to get me through the next day.

I had nearly reached my own floor. My neighbor, Umm Muhammad, was rushing down the stairs clutching an empty pot.

"Not a drop of water since the crack of dawn," she panted as she caught sight of me.

I jammed the key into the rusty lock on the apartment door. It was almost impossible to turn. I shoved the door open with my shoulder and threw the clutch of paper onto the nearest table. I headed for the bathroom, yanked out a bucket and ran down the stairs, swerving around an empty garbage can that a cat was using as a playpen.

When my foot struck the packed dirt of the alley, the falcon eyes were trained on me, waiting.

"'Ulba farigha"
August 1988
Dunya saghira, pp. 57-61

The Shape of Prison

"This is a very early story. You can see the prison inside your head; it has a particular shape. Sometimes it looks like the outline of a certain letter of the alphabet. There is always an exchange going on between our internal prisons and the ones outside. There is an absence of freedom everywhere."

I finished reading the morning paper. I folded it in half and slapped it onto the table nearest my favorite chair. That paper is controlled by the government, anyway.

One last sip of coffee.

I got to my feet, the headache producing a dull pain. I braced myself and twisted the doorknob.

The stairs reeled. I made it to the nearest pharmacy and bought some tranquillizers. From the grocer's, I phoned the office to call in sick. At home, I took a pill and tried to doze but it was no use.

I felt sick to my stomach and I ran to the bathroom. There I found it, in the mirror over the sink, confronting me: a deformed alphabetic shape, a letter that was large, ugly, scarred and pockmarked, inside a barred window frame of caked black ink.

I peered through the tiny, squarish holes in the thick blackness. I saw the sun tucked into a corner, mourning the murdered dream in the children's eyes. I saw the birds huddled inside the bushes refusing to trill.

I came nearer. I saw figures settling helmets over their heads, picking up clubs. Their rough feet trampled the corpses of those

75

they had killed in the streets and tiny lanes, so that the cracking of bones made a continuous groan that sounded most like muffled thunder.

I saw firebombs, houses torn from their roots, a man talking to himself, about himself, another tearing off all his clothes and pissing in a public square, a little girl killing herself from grief.

My legs and arms were trembling. The blood seemed to go hard and dry in my veins. I screamed, made a fist, and aimed it at the blackness. I came out of my confusion to find blood running over the basin, and scattered across the floor I saw razors, glass from the mirror, toothpaste and soap.

I turned away. I made an effort to collect myself, to contain my alarm. I opened the bathroom door and ran, knocking into the walls of my home. The splashes of blood dripping from my hand were spreading.

The twisted letter shadowed me: across the wall the floor the ceiling the tables and chairs and curtains, even the doorknobs and window grips, it tried to grab me, pursuing my small portion of the present, attaching itself to my narrow span of time.

I didn't have the strength to stand. When I woke up on the floor, I found its shape on the wall, clasping my shadow.

"Al-Sajn fi'l-huruf"
February 1979
Dunya saghira, pp. 63-67

The Handsomest Portrait
She Had Ever Seen

"The rapidity of these economic and social transformations we are living through in Egypt is simply incomprehensible to a lot of people. They cannot find a way to grasp the space between their memories and what they see around them. There was so much pride in the social accomplishments of the Nasser years, and Nasser's policies made it possible for people to hope: there were the rent control laws, the free education. Now, for the young people, it is all higra, *outmigration in search of wages, so that one can buy a refrigerator, or bread. You can't return to what was, but you can't see what is ahead, either. The mind stops here."*

Winter nights have no end.

She pushed away the coverlet and sat hunched, squeezing her knees to her chest, her hand on her cheek. The regular rhythm of the alarm clock was keeping her from sleep.

The room was tiny, and clothes lay in heaps on top of the bed and thrown over the chairs. There were papers scattered across the desk and beneath it too. A strong light fell across the wall opposite her bed: the glint in President Nasser's eyes, the broadness of his smile.

It was the handsomest portrait of him she had ever seen. Of course she was accustomed to so many different pictures of him, printed in the newspapers, suspended in streets and squares, hanging on the walls of schools and universities, on the pages of albums, in hospitals. President Nasser, everywhere.

Nasser until the last breath: thus was he. Thus had she gazed at him throughout her childhood and teenage years.

She spoke to him.

"Are you happy with the way things are? You laugh and you stare up into the sky. Do you know the latest news? The owner of the building wants to raise the rent. Would he have dared to do that when you were around?"

She continued.

"Go on, now, *shaykh*, get out of my sight, God pay you back! You got us dreaming, you did, and now we don't know our heads from our feet."

She studied his wide forehead and the brown eyes.

"Even so, you're such a fine cuss! But, don't let it get to you—everything runs its course."

"You're talking to yourself."

She looked up. He bent over her head and she moaned lightly as she pounded her chest.

"O Lord, O Protector—how long have *you* been here?"

He jumped onto the bed, smiling and ready to tease her.

"You tell me first—who's the guy who is such a fine cuss, mmm—ooh handsome, hey good-looking!"

She shoved him away. "Okay, that's enough now—show some manners!"

She wrapped a shawl around her shoulders.

"What kept you up this late?"

"I'm worried." His voice was faint now.

She studied his features—such a mix they were. He'd gotten his late father's darkness and height, and the arched eyebrows he'd taken from his grandfather. From her he had his wide black eyes and from her brother the thick hair. Handsome he was, but so gloomy. That was what her heart felt, but she waited for him to bring up the subject. With her, she knew, he usually did.

He covered his face with his palms.

"I don't know, mama, I just can't decide. Should I go, and leave you alone, or should I wait? Stay here and bring in just pennies?"

It hadn't been so very long since she had been expecting this moment, but still, she had been dreading it. Yet she was used to accepting what she couldn't escape, wasn't she? Her gaze roamed the room. She noticed how the splotches of leaking dampness had broadened in the high corners, and she could see the worn edges of the rug that her mother had given her on her wedding night. She avoided Nasser's face. It was almost dawn. She turned her head, to meet his dulled eyes, evacuated by the light.

"What do *you* want?"

He drew a deep breath.

"Frankly, you mean? And you won't get mad?"

"I won't get mad," she echoed, carefully watching him and waiting.

"To go. But I won't be away from you for very long, a year maybe, or two, not more."

These were the same words she had heard from her brother, and he had spent long years absent until she had grown weary of counting. He came closer, bent towards her.

"What did you say?" he asked.

Her voice could barely be heard. "Whatever you think."

Impatient, he shouted. "You mean, it's okay with you?"

She nodded. His eyes grew bright and he jumped off the bed, speaking loudly, excitedly.

"Quick, I'd better go sleep, just an hour or so, so I'll have the whole day, bright and early."

He stopped suddenly. "Oh, I forgot." He pressed a quick kiss on her head.

"Sleep well, handsome."

Sleep was having its argument with her, and the winter … its night was so heavy. The cold oozed into her weak bones. She stretched out, pulled the blanket up over her chest, stole a glance at Nasser, saw him looking at the sky, and covered her face, muttering.

"Everything runs its course."

"Ajmal sura ra'atha"
1997
Al-Thaqafa al-jadida, no. 114 (March 1998), pp. 103-104

Rape

"It was such an intimate town. There were palms all along the shore-line, and a lake. The asphalt massacred them. Even nature cannot withstand the transformations of Infitah. *It transforms spirits. Dreams, even."*

I always thought of them as entwined plaits of iron perforated by diminutive round punctures.

Every day I walked along the densely constructed metal wall that encircled the wharf. The quay floated quietly, resting on the surface of the water, in the foremost part of the harbor not far from where the boats put down anchor. I could see a semicircle of little white fishing boats that looked just like the paper boats I used to play with when we were little—me, my brothers, and the sons of the neighbors.

Every day, from outside of that wall, I filched a few glances through those tiny round windows. Some of the drivers who were usually perched on the edge of the wall stung me with their stares.

Five minutes from the wharf wall to the group taxi stand, and I'm allowed nothing but a tiny droplet of a look. My eye runs ahead of my gasping stride, and my hopeful thoughts fall away from me, flattened under my worn-out shoes.

The days went by, days in which I counted off some of the boats and nearly figured out how to describe the exact color of the seagulls.

I descended the steps to the town slowly, deliberately, and the streets flirted with my feet.

Today the image will come together in my mind: a high screen of dust, little mountains of pebbles and wood, wires, a bulldozer, hoes and pickaxes, bags of sand. Two foreigners, one tall and blond and the other stocky, wearing thick glasses. They talk in a language I don't understand.

Scattered words from the mouths of drivers sitting on the edge of the wall.

My mind wanders. They will get rid of the boats we used to play with. They will block the breeze that the departing gulls left behind. They will fill in the harbor and dry up the water. Will they truly dry up the water?

My fingertips, feeble as they are, work to unlace the iron plaits. But it's no use at all.

I clutched at the metal wall. I shook it with both hands.

My eyes clung even harder to the tiny windows. I felt dizzy.

I turned, dragging my feet in the direction of the taxis, rivers of salt dampening my lips, the last droplet of my vision evaporating.

"Ightisab"
September 1982
Dunya saghira, pp. 87-88

Everyday Duty

"When feelings turn into a closed drawer, in a desk, within a building, an institution that opens its doors only by appointment ....
"The bond between freedom and emotions is very strong. You cannot really have one without the other."

S he gathered the stray ends of her hair, floating every which way from her face. She picked up the mulberry leaves that had drifted to the ground. Her heart pounded, her chest rose and fell, the sweat lay choking beneath her pores.

She rested her bare back against the bedframe. The faint gleam of the nightlight reflected that moment's shadow in the mirror. Their bodies looked gigantic, the features altered.

He lit a cigarette.

"You don't want it any more."

She moved nearer and lay her hand on his sweating back.

"How can I call back what the years have snatched away?"

He tossed away the cigarette butt.

"Just another excuse."

It was past midnight. She remembered that she had last bought milk several days ago. That the garbage man would come pounding on the door, and possibly give up in disgust. That she wasn't sure she had set the alarm to get her up in time for work.

She turned to him, her eyes on his, but they looked away from each other immediately. She lay down on her back and seized his hands, trying to pull him toward her. Her eyes moved between his naked chest and the cluster lying motionless in the sprouting grass. She tried again. His eyes watched her, watched her, his body frozen. She searched her memory for sensitive regions, ticklish places. Her repeated tries roused a few sleeping feelings. He grabbed the peeled fruit, licked the swelling pomegranate seeds. The cluster dissolved, submerged in the regular cadence of snoring.

She felt a light pricking inside. Breathing with difficulty, she tied back her hair and dried her sweat.

She had drunk in the wine of passion time after time until the leaves of her own autumn had begun to fall and the days became nothing more than burdensome everyday duties. She remembered that it was time to buy a packet of sleeping pills. The old one was empty.

She put the pillow over her head. She begged sleep to come to her. It might break the confining bonds of her own span of time and bring back the remnant of the dream, the passion, that had been.

"Al-Wajib al-yawmi."
Cairo, 1994.
Ibda', 12 no. 9, September 1995, pp. 50-51.
Nakhb iktimal al-qamr, pp. 79-52.

Threads of Thought

"Children, limbs... so many things get broken, and they are not easy to fix. It is hard to practice the same kind of freedom once things have been broken. And so often these feelings remain imprisoned inside."

I picked up the empty glass, filled it, poured half out. I stared at the little disk inside, watching its orange body fizz into spreading bubbles. The circle was wasting away; now the disk was a tiny crescent moon. One gulp. The remnants stayed on my outstretched tongue. I studied it with a half-closed eye, surprised by its new tint.

I pulled the kitchen door shut behind me. The living room was smaller, more cramped than it had been yesterday. The sponge-rubber chair swallowed me. When I sneezed, the bones in my back sent a sharp pain through my body.

The hands of the clock move round.

The face of the tipsy sailor chuckles at me from the wall directly opposite my chair. You can see his eyes shimmer even though they are almost completely shrouded in deep wrinkles. He holds a tankard in one hand and grasps a bottle of rum in the other. His white beard flows cheerfully from his face that—no matter where you are—laughs right into yours.

I had been coming home from work. On the orchard grass directly across from the harbor, the young fellow who sells things right off the harbor boats was laying out some prints he had just acquired. I remember that particular day: I remember kicking my shoes off. I recall the tickly feel of barely wet dirt on my skin. Even the exhaustion of hours of work could not erase that sensation. The other two women, workmates of mine, were looking on from a distance. Their eyes took in the pictures of naked women (suitable for bedrooms) and the prints of assorted plates and bowls filled with fruit destined for dining room tables.

For that moment I followed the whispering of what I felt inside: the yearning in my trusting eyes running toward the eyes of the old sailor, drinking from their warmth.

The clock hands move round. I hear the sound of my child turning restlessly in bed, snuggling into his kitten, his warmth against loneliness. A few days ago he snatched her —and her piteous, broken mewing—right from the street. She wasn't even a month old, I don't think. After some negotiation I agreed that he could bring in a cardboard carton from the trash-filled empty lot behind our home, fill it with sand, and put it in a corner of the kitchen to meet her needs.

His closed bedroom door is cloaked by an immense picture of a young mother, her face bright with health. Her rich brown hair splashes over a short-sleeved blouse. She holds a child closely, a child with laughing eyes.

Although it was some distance from the chair to the door and I wasn't wearing my glasses, my heart read the lines that wandered into one another.

"To mama, on her birthday ... Happy Birthday, and many more, and..." The pains in my back let up. His cradle became a river and my heart unfurled, a white sail piloting him through its waters, and over the unfolding horizons.

The mingled smells of anesthetic and sterilized cotton billowed from the artificial limb. It was over there: a leg propped against the back of the chair drawn up to the desk. The windows were coated with a blue that distorted the view outside.

"Surgery—it has to be surgery. Where is her husband?"

My mother's tears spilled and it was my brother who answered, his voice stumbling.

"Can I take the responsibility? Is that possible?"

"Possible? Of course. Anything is possible in such circumstances," said the doctor. He signaled the nurse to follow him out.

Somewhere beyond those blue windows—but none of us had any idea of where he might be, out among the air-raid sirens.

The blue became part of the woodwork, just another color. The synthetic leg became my inseparable companion for the nights that went on and on.

The clock hands move and the silent moments mouth what cannot possibly be spoken.

I leaned my head against the chair back. I took a deep breath and let it out toward a picture hanging on the wall opposite the leg. A portrait of two naked children, hands clasped, sprouting from a patch of close green. An open sky, an endless open sky.

The roosters' squalling, birds singing, the first bicycle on the street—announcements of daytime, sneaking in around the tiny globes of dew, whispering to the earth, "Make room."

The clock struck six. I straightened the shawl over my chest, stood up quickly, pushed open the kitchen door with my shoulder, took the box of matches from the top of the cupboard, lit one, and got the burner going.

I yanked the milk jug off its peg, emptied the little plastic milk container into it, and began to make breakfast for the boy before he left for school.

"Tuda'iyyat saghira"
Port Saïd 1986
Al-Nawras, pp. 47-51

Open Wound

"We may have been hardheaded, the Nasser generation, but we were romantics too. And it was all shattered by political oppression, and by the defeat of our nation and people. Everyone from this generation suffers still. We thought our dreams were simple, but we learned that they lay beyond our grasp. We are still trying to understand."

- 1 -

"He doesn't have a place to call home, no income, nothing left to him," she snapped.

"We have a long life ahead of us, Mama."

She contorted her mouth. "Death and destruction. Jackass!"

And so she skipped and scampered on with him, skirting the years, dodging the eyes of those who were ready to pounce. In secret she sipped tenderness, watched by the black cats of the passing days, ready to spring, crouched low, waiting, waiting.

- 2 -

"It's all he carries inside him—poems, and love for others."

"We shall see," came the government investigator's acid reply. She gave him a sharp look.

"Our love, our passion, it will go on in spite of you all—you and your so-proud noses in the air, sniffing us out."

He jabbed his finger between her eyes.

"Just watch out, he's still dirt under our feet."

- 3 -

The walls closed in on her and plugged whatever escape routes her heart might have had.

"Who will open the auction of blood?" she screamed. "Who will be first to plunge in the knife?"

Have I not told you, my grieving love, of the eyes staring from behind the windows, watching from behind closed doors. Have I not told you about the cats, ready to pounce?

She wrapped his face in her open palms. She embraced him in her air of distress.

"Why can I still hear the defeat in your voice?" she whispered. "Why have the words in your eyes gone dull?"

He turned his back, leaving impenetrable emptiness behind.

The days: an open wound. Nothing to dress and soothe its fire but the dear one's heart. Passion ensnared in a trap of sorrow.

Her eyes clutched at the horizon.

The frail breath departed her chest to circle tightly overhead. It scrabbled a passageway, for maybe the winds would follow, bearing years of passion to come.

"Al-Jarh al-maftuh"
Cairo 1992
Nakhb iktimal al-qamar, pp. 53-56

Songs from the Tree's Core

"Amidst the pressures of life we do not always listen to the beauty we carry inside. And sometimes folk stories help us hear ourselves."

The images of the tent, the she-camel, and the caravan evoke the pre-Islamic Arabic ode, an important source of pride and inspiration to Arab writers ever since. Often these long poems took the male lover's grief-stricken vision of his beloved's abandoned campsight as opening motif, followed by the motif of journeying.

I told my lucky star about my state of mind and how I longed for a sense of peace. It shook out its feathers, beat its wings and rose over the waters to circle here, circle there, above cities so close, cities distant. It spiraled over the roofs of buildings, upward and against the rain, the winds. It bored through the thunder, waded across a rainbow, and came back exhausted, wings clipped. My lucky star buried its head in my cupped palms and was mute.

I poked my walking stick under my arm and told it of my poor star's trials. It gave its word to bring back my lost, roving mind. It threatened to bring my wits prostrate and humble before me.

It went out in my company, slapping the streets right and left. The cars and trucks crowded it. Their exhaust and incessant clanging encased it.

I shut my ears to the repeating thuds. My walking stick quivered, jerked, and turned into a flying broomstick. I clung to its tail end until it flung me into the desert's soft stomach. A grain among the vagrant sands: before I knew it, that's what I was.

Of my grief I wove my tent. No she-camel, not for me. No bird, no dog to trail a caravan.

I threw myself down full length on the threshold of my eye. I told it of my stifled heart and of the cane that had abandoned me.

It gave me leave to come in. Only me. I crept across the sill as far as I was allowed, right to the rim of the pupil. I stared into its beguiling disk.

I saw a man whose eyes gave cradle to the sun. He scattered seeds all across the ground, and as he did so he sang. And I saw a luxuriant tree. As he sought its shade, it formed a young woman whose laughter diffused musk and perfume. The force of her beauty opened his chest and the pulse of his heart wound around her. His heartbeat was a gentle flute in the hands of its master, so weighed down by the sadnesses he discloses. He unrolled a mat of longings beneath the feet of his little princess.

I ran, my heart free and happy, toward the fragrance of perfume, to the songs. As I came near, the tree and the young woman and the man who sang to the tones of the flute all vanished.

I stood as still as if the ground had pinned me. I lamented my state and my mind's exodus. An old, old woman passed me by: an ancient woman whose eyes pierced time and destiny, leaning on her stick that had once been a living snake.

"He's here, he waits for you," she whispered.

Then on she glided, the flute's voice tracing her path. I turned and looked all around me. Nothing. I called out to her.

"Wait! Wait for me!"

My eyes grew watery. They expelled me from their magic circle. I perched on the threshold, raving.

"The djinni must have touched my mind, or maybe it is the mirage. Or my thirst."

The old woman came back to me: the ancient woman whose eyes pierce time and destiny. Her stick, once a serpent, touched my chest.

"He's here, he waits for you," she repeated.

I came to my senses. I saw a tree in full leaf casting its songs into my heart. And a man my blood knows well, winking, winking only at me. Youths, and women following their children, all laughing, stretching out their hands. To me.

"Al-Ghina' fi asl al-shajara"
Cairo, 1994
Nakhb iktimal al-qamr, pp. 43-47

Pangs

For Isma'il al-Adli
    and for dear ones lost so quickly

*"I dedicated this story to an old friend who returned after a long ab-
sence. But I kept postponing the visits that he and his wife urged. I was
just too busy. After his death, I made that visit. I still had the map he
had made me, in his own hand. I followed it. To mourn."*

The news came. But she knew it was wrong.
She ran. The steel contraption stopped her. She jammed the
ticket in, and when the machine rotated she turned with it, aware
from the whistle's screech that the metro was close by.

"The streets broaden out yet they grow cramped, close. You
and I, two among the crowds, calling out phrase after phrase. Our
hearts blaze, for they are little but bold. Our hands intertwine, and
scrabble and cling to the walls that come between us. And we dream
of a better tomorrow."

The metro car flung her out at his home, the new one. He had
drawn her a little map.

"So you live somewhere near the moon?" she had wailed, fum-
ing. Too many details, too much explanation.   .

His soft eyes laughed, then, and calmed her down. A sense of
security engulfed her, as he patted her on the shoulder.

"The moon? No—they reached *that* a long time ago."

95

At the junction they had stopped. He was going south and she would turn back, riding as far north as she could go.

There. There was the cigarette kiosk where he always bought the brand he liked best. There was the corridor of trees with the tangle of old roots and the interlocked branches, reaching to canopy the street. There were the low-lying buildings, each one like the next, gardens wedged in among them. It was all exactly as the scrap of paper in her hand said.

"The door is always open to you. Come any time, any time at all."

Aah, my dear. I am always late. And, as usual, I have left behind a cup still full of cold tea. As usual, the light stabbing in my heart will not stop.

She came right to the house. His familiar face gazed out at her. She reached out her hand to touch him. It dropped into the emptiness.

She knocked on the door. No one there to answer.

She knocked, hard. She heard the echo. It came, the echo of death.

"Al-Wakhz"
Cairo, 1995
Nakhb iktimal al-qamar, pp. 67-70

Fire

"Lebanon. The war in the south. How long will the world ignore it?"

I picked up my pen, exasperated and ashamed by this self that continuously abandoned me. "My greetings to you, and..." I murmured the words, hoping they would sound better out loud. My mind wandered in the yellow pallor of the walls and among the heaped bills.

A fly circled round the rough plastic carafe that held water. I stared at the books lined up on the desk. Some I had read, others not yet. At this particular moment I could not recall a single thing I had ever read. Anyway, I didn't think the books that were left were in good enough condition to sell.

Words, words. I say them over and over. There are better ones, no doubt, in the Arabic language, ones that would be of more help in trying to secure a loan from a rich sister. But maybe even their magical content would have no effect, so poor was their fit with my life. And an ill fit it had been for so long, this life of mine that merged with hers yet clashed with it to the very core.

I twirled the radio dial. With some diligent effort, I got a distant station. I brought the radio close to my ear, close enough to pick up the number of killed and wounded in the south of Lebanon. Then I prepared myself, just in case I should encounter the thief who had stolen my prescription glasses. From all the glasses in that accursed bus, he had chosen mine. I wanted to be ready to belt him one, to measure out blows enough to bloody his face.

I tried it out loud again. "My greetings to you, and..." Had I come down with some disease? Perhaps it was a disability associated with writing, a bit like the problem that had struck my father at seventy. In his prime, my mother had never spoken above a whisper in his presence. But after it happened, her voice got louder and louder.

Maybe I should go out, I thought. I needed a doctor. Yes, I definitely needed a doctor. Some extra work, too.

I was at the front door, which even at that hour was still barred by its rust-covered bolt, when a question suddenly struck me. If medicine was so clever at curing that kind of impotence, was it advanced enough to treat a writing disease?

I turned away from the door. I threw my jacket down onto the bed and threw myself there after it. But I could not sleep for an irregular sobbing in my heart. Day broke to the voice of the announcer, coming from a far-away station. Katyusha missiles. They were coming down on the enemy's north front.

I hoped the fire would go on forever. Let it happen. Let things take their course, whatever that was. Even if the sobbing in my heart might never stop. Even if the doctor might find me no cure.

"Al-Nar"
Cairo, 1996
Nakhb iktimal al-qamar, pp. 83-86

Kite Full of Color

"No comment."

The color blue teased the tiny waves. Women's loose trousers clung to their backsides. Boys struck the water and laughed. The small children on the beach screamed to the rhythm of their leaps.

Migrating flocks of birds brushed the horizon, and the colorful kites rose higher and higher above the sea.

What did she think of the groom who was to come, her older brother asked. She turned her face toward the open window.

Her mother implored her. "Say yes, God give you guidance, people have been making me feel so ashamed. What on earth am I going to tell them?"

She fixed her eyes on the corridor between the bedroom and the parlor.

"Tell them... tell them I love the nomadic life, and drinking beer, and staying up late on hot summer nights."

Her mother shouted, sparks flying from her eyes. "You'll be an old maid before you know it—now say 'God willing.'"

"Say you'll go through with the engagement, at least," added her brother. "Then maybe..."

He chose an umbrella some way down the beach. He stretched out on the chaise longue. He rubbed her thigh.

"Your body is mine. Only mine."

He was wearing a suit, the necktie tight enough to shorten his breath. When she remained silent, he swung his head toward her. She noticed the little white hairs that sat over his forehead and framed his face glistening in the rays of the sun.

He came so close that she could see her face in his dark glasses.

"I want a full report on you, every detail, once a week, every week." His voice was loud.

She closed her eyes on the drumming and dancing of the young women and men enjoying themselves. His mouth almost touched her ear as he whispered.

"I love you, and what happens to you matters to me."

Her tiny dreams crept out of a niche in her memory. Friends and neighbor children falling eagerly on palm stems, colored paper, and lengths of string in the open space that separated their homes. They competed and argued over who had made the best-looking and the fastest-moving kites. And they could keep their little brothers busy, even happy, plaiting the tails their kites would fly.

She ran barefoot over the sand, clutching the very end of the string.

Rising, falling, she raced the kite of her neighbor, who was also her cousin. The sea shared her laughter, her delight at a kite full of color.

When the eyes surrounded her, she shrank in fright; her mother was so insistent. The family instructed her to be more modest, more bashful. So she started wearing the headscarf and long-sleeved blouse, and the hem of her skirt swept the dust of the street.

His raised voice brought her back from her wanderings.

"You're not answering me. Why?"

She tried to get to her feet. The long skirt compressed her inside her body, and she almost tripped. She grabbed hold of the umbrella stem and shouted into his face.

"Hasn't anyone told you? I don't like to stay in one place, I do like drinking beer, and I like to stay up late on hot summer nights."

His eyes grew anxious. The words he was trying to speak wouldn't come out.

She turned her back on him. She yanked off the scarf, freeing her hair to let it flow as the sails on ships did. She undid the top buttons of her blouse and took a deep breath, storing in her chest as much sea air she could.

She ran barefoot on the sand, and a kite full of color raced her shadow.

"Ta'ira mulawwana"
Cairo, 1996
Nakhb iktimal al-qamar, pp. 87-91

Lost Harbor

"This is a very old story. I was still at the university when I wrote it. I thought a lot about harbors."

- 1 -

The harbor revolves round itself, turn after turn, and loses its way on the sea's vast surface, time after time. Its walls wail the burdens of the stranger while its waters bellow at the garbage: patches of oil, remnants of tin cans, illnesses, pestilence.

- 2 -

Sadnesses make the voyage, sadnesses arrive, and the harbor's eyelids never close. Those eyes are ever wakeful, counting off the yield of the years and finding nothing but trifles. Long ago the waters of the sea dwindled; no longer do they bring the wealth and goodness of old. A barren today has swallowed the skies, and they no longer offer the rains.

- 3 -

The drought has carved the lean children thinner. Their legs bow, and the half-moons of black beneath their eyes have deepened. Hunger and death embrace. The earth has swallowed the echo of groaning, and no longer are there children at the harbor.

- 4 -

The men set out on their seafaring way to be flung afar by the winds. Their spirits dissolved in the wombs of the waves.

The women's wailing split the walls of silence, their eyes wakeful, open wide through the nights, probing the summit of the path those men had taken.

Be it but a returnee. Be it a dear one.

"Al-Mina' al-ta'ih"
1974
Al-Thaqafa l-jadida, no. 114 (March 1998), p. 102

Song of the Wounded Heart

Dedicated to the children of the stones, those who confronted the guns of the first *intifada*, in Palestine

"The kernel of this story was a child I saw at a party. He kept tugging at his sleeves, trying to make them stretch down to his wrists. Even children learn the constant inner war against poverty and hunger."

The housing crisis in Cairo is such that in many poor urban households the front room or entree onto which the front door of the apartment opens has to serve multiple purposes. Often it is carved from a larger, probably old, apartment that has been subdivided so that plumbing has had to be jerry-rigged.

Egyptian currency includes 5-piastre, 10-piastre, and 25-piastre bills as well as coins. In other words, a pile of paper currency can amount to very little.

Yesterday it had been her turn to clean the stairway.
He stood in the front room that was also the kitchen and bathroom.

"Aren't you coming with me?"

She bent to hoist the pail.

"I'll catch up with you as soon as I finish here."

For a moment he did not speak. Then she heard a shout. He was riffling through the pile of faded little bills on the wooden table.

"Isn't there any more than this?"

"Take it."

"But you?"

"I'll manage," she said, chopping a cut-rate bar of soap into chunks and tossing them into the pail.

She got as far as the open front door, a small broom under her arm. He caught up with her right at the threshold. "Are you sure Umm Noosa will bring the white shirt so I can change into it before the assembly?"

She set the pail down on the threshold and turned toward him. The shine had gone out of his little eyes, she noticed, and she remembered that she had not been to the store for milk in several days. She was about to rest her dirty palm on his shoulder but instead she drew back and answered him quietly.

"We shook hands on it, and Umm Noosa doesn't go back on her promises. So go on now, safe and sound, my dear, or else you'll be late."

He scurried off, dragging his skimpy shadow behind him. She gazed at the stairway, at each landing and step where the contents of the garbage cans lay, scattered by stray cats during the night.

She tipped the pail and the water flowed, breaking over each step it met.

When she had finished she knocked on her neighbor's door. The youngest daughter answered, the one whose white-pocked face always showed a yellowish tinge.

"My mother went to the market but she should be back anytime."

She called to the neighbor one floor below. The woman's upraised face showed at an angle over the balustrade. She asked for some of what she needed, and the neighbor sent her little boy up with enough to get her through the day.

She arrived slightly after the ceremony had started.

"Wandering stranger, from a nation lost—stranger of the wounded heart."

As their singing grew louder, so did the clapping. The elation shone in the black depths of their eyes. With them she mouthed the words that had quickened her heartbeat. "Wandering stranger..." The children's drawings were hung all across the plaster wall of this old, two-story school building. Her eyes picked out a house and a flower and a child veiled in the flag of his nation, throwing stones. An old woman making a victory sign. Tanks, airplanes, houses made of trees.

She knew very few of the mothers who had come with their children.

He stood far in the back at the very end of the little hall. He glanced in her direction. He looked so dignified up on the little wooden stage, singing solemnly among his classmates. The sleeves of the white shirt, she noticed, were a little shorter on him than they had been on Umm Noosa's son.

She remembered the day her grandmother had told her, "The beetle saw its eggs on the wall and said: 'Why, they're pearls strung on a thread.'"

She didn't care. To her, he looked like a prince bearing a sword of silver. She saw them all, so small. She saw them big. Birds, leaves, flowers, rivers. She saw. The songs burst from their little hearts and souls, and as they came out, they turned into stones.

"Ughniyat al-qalb al-jarih"
November 1987
Dunya saghira, pp. 89-94

Glass Barricades

"The repetition of words creates barriers between me and others. Nothing new happens to sweep the barriers, or the debris, of words away. So often we exist in a state of routine. We let our lives pass in boredom."

And then, once they had begun to talk about so-and-so, and his separation from so-and-so, and then about the man who had caused his friend's ruin, and of the woman who... yes, then I spoke up.

"Whoever among us has the power to know where his foot will fall next is delivered from evil. But to cast the blame on whomever you choose, on this person, that person—no. Perhaps it's just all the little things that have built up. Perhaps it is the pressure. Or...

"Our loved ones, you know, are like water. They slip through our fingers. They slip away before our own eyes. Don't squander your own flesh, don't. And let the final stone fall on your very own house."

Over and over I insisted. Their eyes went glassy. The atmosphere grew chilly. It was as cold as death then, as icy as death in a marble body.

I put my hand out to signal my farewell. My arm reached on, stretched on and on. And my palm struck against the glass barricade.

The sirens. Fangs, snapping at my head. I hurried away, to avoid the crush, the commotion, the night's sudden arrival.

All those letters of the alphabet that we have exchanged. All are depleted. Nothing is left but the borders, etched around empty spaces. The brink, the extreme, of eye to eye. The distance between our time, between now and memory. It is a void that grows.

The weariness that time brings kills. Groans long quelled almost make their escape.

In vain did our hands work to pierce the glass barricade.

"You," I said. "You there—my heart, your house. They are crouched inside. Do not go away. My flesh, your flesh: they do not part."

Eye to eye. Wall beyond wall. Barricades. The hand extending, reaching. Further. The hand. Bearing the first stone toward the house.

"Al-Hawajiz al-zujajiyya"
January 1991
Dunya saghira, pp. 15-16

Nothing At All

Muhammad Fawzi is a popular Egyptian singer. One of his famous songs is "Mama, zamanha gayya," (Mama—she'll be here any time). Fayruz is a famous Lebanese female singer who has been at the forefront of expressing not only the pain and frustration that political oppression and struggle have generated in the Arab world but also the pride that resistance and strong national identities can bring.

She came near. He spread out the tobacco across the sheets of newspaper.

She almost said something to him.

He busied himself rolling his cigarettes and paid no attention to her.

A long silence.

She listened to the neighbors' television.

"Muhammad Fawzi is singing. Must be a Muhammad Fawzi film. I love Muhammad Fawzi," she said.

He did not raise his head.

She chewed on her fingernails.

He inhaled, long and deep, and leaned his head back. He blew out the smoke, and the ceiling absorbed the bluish tint. A gecko fled into the corner.

She left her cold seat.

She turned on the tape player.

"O years now gone, come back to me
Return now once, come back to me
Take me back to childhood's door
And I'll scamper in sunshiny pathways."

The salty drops collected over her heart, bolted fast.
"Years don't return, Fayruz," she whispered. "No years return."
His voice came to her, grating. "Did you say some-
    thing?"
She shut off the tape player. "Nothing. Nothing at all."

"La shay'"
Cairo, 1997
Akhbar al-adab, 1997

Bitter Mirth

"Are we writers or beggars? The bureaucratic slowness of government presses, on which we have to depend, is one way to deter us from publishing. And then there is the material side, which one cannot ignore."

The proverb about the peach pit and the water jug suggests that it is the details of life—those supposedly unimportant matters—that underlie and shape the events that are perceived as more important. The author plays with another popular proverb, "'ala qaddi lihaafak maddid rigleek" (extend your legs as far as your sheet or coverlet reaches). In other words, don't exceed your grasp. The author also exploits the identical sound, in colloquial Egyptian Arabic, of "pain" (alam) and "pen" (qalam), since Cairenes and Delta Egyptians drop the q in most words. She may also be playing on a double colloquial meaning of qalam, as "pen" and as an insulting term for "slap."

He rapped the nib of his pen against the sheet metal of his desk.

"I've told you—first, I absolutely must follow the procedures, before I do anything else. There's information needed, clerical work, accounts, all that before I can sign your payment voucher."

"Sir, please! Do me a favor... I can't wait any longer—it's too much to bear." His voice was faint.

The man behind the desk jabbed and pulled at his eye with one index finger, stretching the skin until the eye looked distended.

"These are procedures that must be followed, don't you understand that?"

The growing mound of debts stared down at him from the spaces between the tiny letters rotating on the printing presses. He dropped his head and swiveled until his mouth was close to that ear.

"I know that it's your job," he mumbled. "But can't you pay me part of the total amount? It's the little peach pit, you know, that may keep the water jug from tipping."

The man thrust his gray hair and decrepit eyeglasses in among the papers on the desk. He found a ruler and steadied it under the lines, smacking his lips in disapproval.

"There is no strength or power but with God! May the Lord grant me patience."

He lugged his shadow outside. From the moment his eyes had opened to catch their first glimpse of the sun, it seemed, he had been pulling the sheet taut. He had stretched it and stretched it, but never had it been long enough to cover him completely. The pain and the pen bunched themselves up, a single lump in a hollow of his heart. Letters alone could no longer sheathe the stillness he could describe only as bitter mirth.

He turned his back on the crush of people. The despair that had conquered his insides so very long ago, leaving space for nothing else, followed closely behind.

He shot a blank stare at the heaps of rasping flesh in the street, the smoke, and the clouds gathering into another haze.

He hoped fervently for a hard rain.

"Al-Farah al-murr"
Cairo, 1994
Nakhb iktimal al-qamar, pp. 71-74

Short-lived Moments

"When the Americans began to bomb Baghdad again, I could not write. All I could do was fear. The fear, and a complete lack of communication—these are what mark our lives. Everyone tries to live in their own little valley."

I meant to write.
No,
it will be no use,
no use to create a moment out of things replicating themselves
out of faces that all look alike
and the carbon-copy words we say to each other.

I meant to sing.
How,
when my heart is closed around emptiness?

So let me go somewhere, anywhere.
No,
daylight everywhere still…
and the eyes of the shop owner
to whom I owe the cost of my food
trail me
like a swinging pendulum, back and forth,
along the street corners
and to the ends of closed alleys.

I turn the radio dial
to a music hour
and listen
to a quiet tune
as the grief erupts inside
for short-lived moments
with their bitter and their sweet.

A friend's face:
I found her yesterday
as we scurried
after our morsels of bread,
slapped by the coldness of a midwinter month.
We had the usual conversation,
American bombs over Baghdad.
We ask and ask,
Why now?
We listen,
eyes narrowed on
the moment in which the part we played was done.
I turn over the empty coffee cup,
light a cigarette,
study my pen, tossed away, alone,
at the other end of the table.
I reach my fingers toward it
to give it some warmth, inside the paper's heart.

"Awqat 'abira"
Cairo
January 1999
Unpublished manuscript

Passage

"Legends, the Thousand and One Nights, *children's stories—where do our minds travel? Why do we keep certain childhood memories and lose others?" (I.S.)*

"Ya shams ya shammusa" comes from a song that children sing when they lose a baby tooth: "Ya shams ya shammusa, khudi sinnat al-gamusa, wa-hati sinnat al-'arusa!" (Oh sun, dear little sun, take the water buffalo's tooth, and bring the bride's!)

The exchange between storyteller and audience that the storyteller initiates with the words "Bless the Prophet!" signals that the story is about to begin and also involve the audience in the act of storytelling. The folk figure of the ogre or ghoul with a red (inflamed) eye is used in certain popular expressions, notably "Ana hawarriik al-ayn al-hamra," literally, "I'll show you the red eye": that is, "I'm going to make life very difficult for you." Umm al-Dawahi, "Mama Mishap," literally "mother of calamities," is she who can bring on trouble. The epithet implies craftiness, a certain deliberate conjuring of evil. The author associates this figure with stories from the Thousand and One Nights *that she heard from her mother and aunt as a child. The* naddaaha *is a spirit thought to inhabit the nighttime, who calls out to individuals by name. She leads them into the water, heedless, and they drown.*

The rooster paused directly over my head and began to crow incessantly until he could be sure that his squawk had gone right through my eardrum.

"Praise be to God who alone is praised in adversity," I said back. "To God we belong, and to God belongs all sovereignty."

My brain, still submerged in sleep on my bed, remembered; and yesterday I had given him hell. I truly believed he had gone away for good. Yes, though it had made me unhappy and tired me out and given me grief. I had turned it over and over in my mind, tossing this way and that, and to him I'd cried out.

- 1 -

I parted the waters within the sac and dove deeper. My mother trembled hard and let out a shriek. She beat her hands against her breasts, sobbing for her sister, and the midwife bore down, down, so that the boy would come, the boy to follow five girls. Down she pressed and my body convulsed, shrinking from her fingers. There was a fluttering inside my head, as if a tiny bird perched there; and then I burst from the sac, seeking another refuge in escape.

- 2 -

I hung onto the tree of tales. Between my palms, I pressed a sweet pancake. The hoary fox of the woods appeared, dragging himself along on the strength of his feverishness. A cozy bed of pelts that tree might well have been, and the sky a cradle of shadow nibbled by the sun—*ya shams ya shammusa!* the sun of my beloved childhood rhymes. I sang, the contagion crouching beneath the tree forgotten. I sang, not yet gorged with song. My foot slipped with the song, and now the tree reared above me and the elderly shape lay beneath.

- 3 -

"Bless the Prophet!"

"May blessings and peace be upon him," I answered.

"And now bless the Prophet once more!"

"The most bounteous blessings and peace," I said quickly.

"And then, my little princess," said my aunt, "when the angry-eyed ogre wailed, the palaces and farmland quailed. And the little princess—who looked just like you, my princess! With her noble birth and breeding and her golden braid, that princess was not afraid.

"So she resolved, once the ogre was asleep (his snore irked rats and vermin, it was so loud and deep), to steal the key right off the foul creature's neck and open the door to the seventh room—which after the sixth the ogre forbade—and she'd eat the forbidden apple. The ogre changed into a monkey but his eye was still red. It settled on the princess and we know what happened then, and the king complained to the sage of the age, of the mind of the princess, lost and gone once she saw what she saw, once she told the ogre his eye was red."

- 4 -

I ran from vault to vault until I reached the night before the thousandth since birth. Behind me, I had left the prince and the patrol and the rooster that squawks, the soaring stallion, the bride of the waters, and the thick, gloomy night.

I say: "Out from the night before the thousandth crept Umm al-Dawahi, Mama Mishap. As ages passed she concealed herself inside the country's covenants, and, like the evil siren, like the *naddaaha* who takes people into death, she filched and filched the minds of folk."

Mama Mishap said: "As for you, my son Adam, if you hold me down I'll still come to you—in disguise. But if you follow me, I will make you my model and paragon."

After the princes, the sultans, the fame, and the glory, Mama Mishap settled on the throne of time, and divided and multiplied. I opened the chest of the thousand nights; I sat with the sage and the aged fortuneteller, as she pondered the plot I was in.

Said the gray one: "For Mama Mishap to lose her way, her right eye must be plucked and her heart torn from its roots."

I said: "Mama Mishap, should you test your power to deceive, surely God is the Best of Deceivers."

I invoked the Most Beneficent, and from the abundance of humankind I corralled the wise, the worker, and the simple.

- 5 -

We return to the beginning.

After the rooster's crow subsided, my mind rubbed its eyes and stretched full length on the bed. Next to it still there laid the sword, the pen, and the guide.

My mind steadied itself and called on God's protection from the ogre, the hoary fox, Mama Mishap, and the dense, unknowable night.

"Al-Rihla"
Dunya saghira, pp. 5-11

The Boot

The aroma of war lingers in the particulars of things. A small detail might remind us of events we thought we had forgotten with the passage of time, but then our deepest feelings are stirred up, whether consciously or subconsciously. Might our emotions give body to a life in memory that we assumed had vanished forever?

The boot is one of the minutiae of wartime, but it carries the odor of memories. The wife of a long-ago fighter remembers it. He fought in the October 1973 War. Of her absent partner only this aroma remains, embodied in the boot he wore, a boot now unforgettable.

The bus was choked with soldiers. With difficulty she found a place. The smell of the boots, of buried sweat, overflowed the cramped space where she huddled over a white bundle that hung still between her heart and her chest.

The seats were badly worn, the windows gray if they weren't shattered. As the wheels groaned, the driver's eyes swung like a pendulum between the steering wheel and the rust-corroded mirror.

Little Susu. She adjusted the blanket around him, trying to shun the cold air that seeped in through the pocks in the glass. The soldiers were singing and swaying, as some toppled onto others along the bus's narrow aisle.

She undid her knotted handkerchief and wiped the little one's face. She slipped her hand inside her bosom, and beneath the edge of her handkerchief the little one fixed eagerly onto the source of his nourishment, his cry suddenly muted.

Her gaze unfurled across the windowpane. Clouds gathered, pleating into a new fogginess, and the desert's sweep all but swallowed the horizon. Electricity poles, guard boxes, automobiles, and barbed wire raced her eyes and the raucous bus.

Some soldiers who'd been standing in the aisle vaulted onto their seated colleagues, perching so that their heads touched the ceiling. They had cleared a space where one of their mates danced to the beat of their clapping hands and feet and the thudding of empty cans against the exposed metal of back seats.

The night of henna: ululations, songs, and one embrace after another had spread along the night-owl street beneath their home, celebration of the wedding to come. The echoing sea came to them, joyful, and the lighthouse beam turned, above the rooftops, capering in time with the rhythm that rose from below. And he and she danced, intoxicated with a reverie that lay silent in their dreamy eyes.

Her hennaed night—she had not realized—had carried in its belly the seed of separation. It was an autumnal evening when the stars hovered and circled round the moon, a crescent.

She wrapped her shawl around her shoulders and waved with the others standing in the square. He was just exactly as she loved: brown, tall, almond-shaped eyes and a broad forehead, wearing the khaki uniform, those heavy boots and a beret atop his ebony-black, rustling hair. Every day, late in the afternoon, she walked to the harbor. She watched the seagulls and the ferry and the lighthouse beam, and the women whose eyes clung to sails that were nowhere, with children hanging on their long gowns in back while before them hovered the ships departing for distant countries.

That day, late in the afternoon, the sound of shots in the air and the shriek of airplanes took her unawares. She ran, hid herself behind a screen, raised her head, saw the sky the color of blood and the frames of buildings on the other shore falling like leaves from trees.

Terror overcame the children and the women ran, wailing, while the elderly stumbled as they tried to make their way down a street jammed with people escaping their fear and the fires. Flames broke out wildly, a hell on every side, scattering families, friends, each to a different place, and who would care if the dream of returning pelted ceaselessly through one's heart? Each time he came to visit he pulled off his boots and the smell of buried sweat rose, stifled and hidden sweat that with time had intermingled with fumes of their passion. And when he dozed fleetingly, she gazed at the boots parked by the door, her thoughts wandering.

Would she see him again, she wondered?

Her belly was swelling. He would leave and return. Once, and he did not return again.

As the little one fell asleep, she pulled her nipple out gently, and at that moment her troubled eyes met a furtive glance.

The noise died down, sleepy soldiers collapsing into piles. Staring at the bundle curled in her lap, the soldier sitting next to her spoke. "Is someone waiting for you?"

She stared into the face of their little one and nodded.

"Maybe."

He took a great breath. He was young, his features sharply drawn, his face scarred despite his youth.

"His father?"

She bowed her head, silent.

Her feet had split and cracked, for day after day she had dragged them along the asphalt, between military barracks and administrative offices, hospitals, bed frames, the martyred. There was no use.

She ran into black heaps of flesh, fled from groans and slit chests. Her heart sobbed and the tiny mass of rosy flesh she carried shivered as she circled and circled, but there was no answer, no one to return.

His friendly, familiar shadow clung to her wherever she went, and the smell of buried sweat and passion never left her.

He had held her tightly to his chest, reciting his own charm to ward off the years of hardship and attrition. She was a certitude: return to their homes, and the nation's good name.

With a gentle hand the soldier patted the little one, his words coming loudly. "The one who has fathered children has not truly died."

She pushed his hand away. She turned her face away, her heart's conversation enough.

No, no. Alive to gather God's blessing. The trace of delight in her sad heart. Was it possible that he could die?

The smell of iodine pierced the holes in the glass. She knew the bus was close to the sea. There she would meet him. They would take in each other's aroma and hug exactly as they'd done on the night of henna. He would dance, on and on to exhaustion, until he would throw himself into her burning arms.

The odor of iodine woke the soldiers, longing for their sea's wakeful night and the embraces of their own. All of the tumult of the trip returned. The vehicle passed swiftly along the barbed wire and guardboxes, surrounded by buses full to overflowing with returning soldiers who waved and called out.

Little Susu.

She looked into his almond eyes. She laughed, gathering him to her chest after bundling him with care. The soldiers hurried toward the door of home. The smell of hidden sweat became sharper and her feverish passion hung suspended between watchfulness and the boots parked at the door.

Cairo
October 1999

Milton Keynes UK
Ingram Content Group UK Ltd.
UKHW020831050324
438675UK00023B/800